LEARN MISHNAH

LearnMishnah

BY JACOB NEUSNER

BEHRMAN HOUSE, INC.
PUBLISHERS

ACKNOWLEDGMENTS My thanks go to those who shared in making this book: Linda Altshuler, copy-editor; David Altshuler, coordinating editor; Ed Schneider, designer; Rabbi Joel Zaiman, Rabbi Alvin Kaunfer, Professor Richard S. Sarason, advance readers and helpful critics; Suzanne Neusner, wife.

J. N.

Library of Congress Cataloging in Publication Data
Neusner, Jacob
  Learn Mishnah.

  SUMMARY: Introduces Mishnah, the oral law of Judaism received by Moses from God at Mount Sinai.
  1. Mishnah—Study—Text-books. [1. Mishnah. 2. Jewish religious education] I. Title.
BM497.8.N476   296.1'23'06   78-5482   ISBN 0-87441-310-9
ISBN13: 978-0-87441-310-6

For
Tzvee Zahavy

PREFACE

Mishnah is the oral half of the whole Torah revealed by God to Moses, our rabbi, at Sinai. Mishnah is part of Torah. God gives Torah day by day, and the important things in Torah are important because they talk to us about the world we know. When we say a blessing before and after we read the Torah in the synagogue, we say . . . .נוֹתֵן הַתּוֹרָה—*who gives the Torah*—meaning here and now. By our presence *we receive the Torah,* here and now. This book is meant to help you receive and accept, make use of, the Torah in the concrete and everyday world you know. It is not about the past and in no way concerns a book which came down to us from a particular place or time in history. It is about God's revelation which God *gives* day by day, and which, as I said, we *receive* day by day. If Mishnah is not that, if Mishnah merely is a work out of "Jewish history," then Mishnah is not worth your time and attention. For what makes all the effort required to master this difficult book worthwhile is not that it is a monument to a dead past, but that it is an urgent challenge to the living present, to you and to me.

I dedicate this book to my former student, Tzvee Zahavy, who combines a love for Torah, in its fullest and deepest sense, with a life of loyalty to all the *misvot.* He is a teacher of Judaism and a teacher whose lessons are to be learned by watching what he does, not merely hearing what he says. I love him and take pride in his achievements.

J. N.

Contents

PART ONE

What is Mishnah?

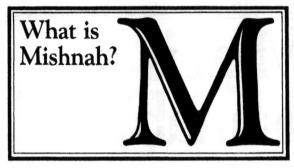

What is Mishnah?

ishnah is a book of rules, put together by Judah the Patriarch, the head of the Jews of the Land of Israel, in about the year 200 of the Common Era. It consists of six major parts, orders, which are called in Hebrew סְדָרִים. Each of the six parts is divided into large tractates, called in Hebrew מַסֶּכְתּוֹת, and each tractate is divided into chapters, called in Hebrew פְּרָקִים.

Mishnah is important for a simple reason. From the time that Judah the Patriarch published the Mishnah to the present time, Jews have regarded Mishnah as a holy book, that is, a book which contains the things God wants us to know. In fact, they have called Mishnah *torah*, and they have believed that Mishnah is part of the Torah of Moses, received from God at Mount Sinai. When we study Mishnah, therefore, we learn things God wants us to know, just as when we study the Bible, we learn God's will for Israel, the Jewish people. Mishnah is half of the Torah received by Moses at Mount Sinai, and the other half is the written Torah we call תַּנַ"ךְ.

In fact, Judaism is based on the two Torahs. The written one we call תַּנַ"ךְ and the other one is passed on not in writing but by memory. It is wrong to think that Judaism and תַּנַ"ךְ are one and the same. Judaism is the religion of Torah, and Torah is in two parts, the written, תַּנַ"ךְ, and the oral, מִשְׁנָה. Only when the two are put together do we have the complete message that God gives to Israel, the Jewish people.

In this book we will learn a number of passages of Mishnah. We shall ask the same questions of each passage: What does it mean? How is it put together? Why is it relevant to me? But, to begin with, we learn a passage of Mishnah that tells us what Mishnah says about itself. Let's begin our first Mishnah.

MISHNAH ABOT 1:1

The first thing you'll want to know is the meaning of the title of this unit.

Mishnah is familiar. *Abot* is the name of the tractate of Mishnah in which our unit is found. Then comes *1:1*. The first *1* is the number of the chapter. The second *1* is the number of the paragraph in the chapter. So *Mishnah Abot 1:1* is 1. a unit of *Mishnah*, 2. tractate *Abot*, 3. the first *chapter*, 4. the first *paragraph*.

Here we learn what Mishnah is. But our unit never refers to Mishnah. It speaks instead of "torah" with a small t and says that Moses received *torah* at Sinai. What is *torah*? It is truth which God tells us. And since the *torah* of which our Mishnah speaks is not the written Torah alone, it follows that our Mishnah speaks of that other torah, the Torah which is learned by memory.

We go through two steps to learn Mishnah. First, we read the Mishnah as it is. We must know the meaning of each and every word in our Mishnah. Second, we read the Mishnah again, this time the way it is put together, line by line, so we learn how the Mishnah is constructed and how it works. Each Mishnah is a little poem. First we read the Mishnah and make certain we know the meaning of its words. Second we read the Mishnah to learn its meaning as a poem.

How the Mishnah Is Put Together

מֹשֶׁה קִבֵּל תּוֹרָה מִסִּינַי וּמְסָרָהּ לִיהוֹשֻׁעַ, וִיהוֹשֻׁעַ לִזְקֵנִים,
וּזְקֵנִים לִנְבִיאִים, וּנְבִיאִים מְסָרוּהָ לְאַנְשֵׁי כְנֶסֶת הַגְּדוֹלָה. הֵם
אָמְרוּ שְׁלֹשָׁה דְבָרִים: הֱווּ מְתוּנִים בַּדִּין, וְהַעֲמִידוּ תַלְמִידִים הַרְבֵּה,
וַעֲשׂוּ סְיָג לַתּוֹרָה.

Vocabulary

received	קִבֵּל	prophets	נְבִיאִים
from Sinai	מִסִּינַי	they handed it	מְסָרוּהָ
handed it on	מְסָרָהּ	men of	אַנְשֵׁי
elders, sages	זְקֵנִים	synagogue	כְנֶסֶת

the great	הַגְדוֹלָה	raise up	הַעֲמִידוּ
three	שְׁלֹשָׁה	disciples	תַלְמִידִים
things	דְּבָרִים	many	הַרְבֵּה
be	הָווּ	make	עֲשׂוּ
patient	מְתוּנִים	fence	סְיָג
judgment	דִּין		

How the Mishnah Is Put Together

Moses received Torah from Sinai	1 מֹשֶׁה קִבֵּל תּוֹרָה מִסִּינַי
and he handed it on to Joshua	2 וּמְסָרָהּ לִיהוֹשֻׁעַ,
and Joshua to elders	3 וִיהוֹשֻׁעַ לִזְקֵנִים,
and elders to prophets	4 וּזְקֵנִים לִנְבִיאִים,
and prophets handed it on to the men of the great synagogue	5 וּנְבִיאִים מְסָרוּהָ לְאַנְשֵׁי כְנֶסֶת הַגְּדוֹלָה.

bot, 'Fathers', is the part of Mishnah which tells us what Mishnah is. Abot contains the sayings of 'Fathers'—founders—of Torah. These teachings are the *torahs* that all together form Torah. Abot begins with this sentence:

Moses received Torah from Sinai.

Notice that it does *not* say, "Moses received *the* Torah," but Moses received *Torah*. Why? Because Torah is open-ended and stands for teaching, instruction, important lessons, which to begin with come from God. Mishnah

6

begins with the claim that Moses received Torah—received *torah*, teaching, from God.

The sentence continues:

> *And he handed it on to Joshua, and Joshua to the sages, and sages to the prophets, and prophets handed it on to the men of the great synagogue.*

The claim is now spelled out. Moses received *torah*. He passed it on to Joshua, and Joshua passed it on, and the people to whom he gave it also passed it on.

Mishnah is the half of the Torah that Moses passed on, not in writing but by speaking to Joshua, and Joshua passed on that part of Torah, not in writing but by telling it to the great sages, and so on for many years.

The first sentence—*Moses received torah at Sinai*—is the most important statement in the whole Mishnah. Yet it says nothing that we do not know from the Bible itself—that Moses received instruction, teaching, at Sinai. But what does that simple sentence claim? It claims that truth comes to us from God who made heaven and earth. What is it that God wants us to know?

1. The first thing is that God wants us to know something.
2. The second is that what God wants us to know is in the word *torah*.
3. The third is that God gives us Torah that contains *torah*—and for us, that is *not* a silly saying. There are truths that we know because God tells them to us.

So far as Mishnah is concerned, we are going to find out the kinds of teachings—torahs—truths that add up to Torah, the sorts of information they give us, and the things we are supposed to have in our minds because of the tremendous, world-shaking event of Sinai.

LET'S LEARN MISHNAH—LET'S SING MISHNAH.

Now memorize the sentence: *Moshe qibbel torah missinai.* Why?

Because that's how Moses did it. If you want to enter into Mishnah, to become part of its world, you must first do what the people who wanted to learn Mishnah always have done. Mishnah is learned by memory because

Mishnah was received by Moses and not written down. We have to imitate Moses. Only then can we claim to know what it is to learn Mishnah the way it is learned by Jewish people. But how easy it is to learn these four heavy words:

Moshe qibbel torah missinai.

It is not hard. And it is easier if you *say* it out loud, and easier still if you make up a song to sing it. How many notes are there? Count the syllables.

There are nine. Have you ever sung a Jewish sentence? Of course you have, at the *Passover Seder:*

Mah nishtanah hallailah hazzeh

Count the syllables, and you come to the same number:

mah   nish— tan—nah   hal—lai—lah   haz—zeh
mo — she   qib—bel   to — rah   mis—sin—nai

So sing the sentence the way you sing the first sentence of the Four Questions.

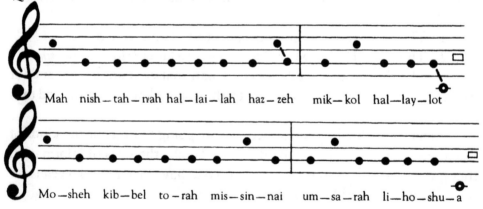

Mah   nish—tah—nah hal—lai—lah haz—zeh   mik—kol hal—lay—lot

Mo—sheh kib—bel to—rah mis—sin—nai   um—sa—rah li—ho—shu—a

Why ignore the words and pay attention, instead, to the music? Because if you want to learn Mishnah, you have to sing. And we can learn to sing a tune and then put different words to it. Our tune is the one we know from the *Passover Seder,* and the tune must be completed. And so it is.

And the meaning also is completed.

1. Moses *received.*
2. Moses *passed on.*
3. *To* Joshua.

Those three things: 1. *receive*, 2. *pass on*, 3. *to* someone.

From here on, you can use the old tune for the Four Questions, or you can make up your own. Sing whatever helps you memorize.

Now we have a story of three steps by which *torah* goes from God to Moses and the people of Israel, and the three steps are matched by three sayings. It's easy to remember *threes*. This set of three is not hard to explain. We have three steps in the handing on of Torah:

1. Joshua to elders—wise people. The first step in handing on Torah is to give it to people who will understand it.

2. Wise people to prophets. Prophets are people who are more than wise. They know more than how things work from day to day. Prophets have insight. They know how things are going to work; they can look deeply into the world as we know it and see where the world will be heading if it keeps up this way.

3. And the prophets gave it to the whole group, the great assembly of all Israel.

Torah is not something for wise people alone, nor will it serve only the people who can see where things are heading. Torah matters—*torah* becomes Torah—only when it is in the hands of all of Israel, the whole Jewish people.

Because when God gives Torah to Moses, God gives *torah* through Moses, through the faithful disciple of Moses—Joshua—through the students of Joshua—sages—through the thinkers who worked out the meaning of what Joshua told sages—the prophets—and it all ends up in the hands of the whole of Israel.

THE THREE SAYINGS

They said three things	הֵם אָמְרוּ שְׁלֹשָׁה דְבָרִים:
1. Be patient in judgment	הֱווּ מְתוּנִים בַּדִּין,
2. Raise up many disciples	וְהַעֲמִידוּ תַלְמִידִים הַרְבֵּה,
3. Make a fence for the Torah	וַעֲשׂוּ סְיָג לַתּוֹרָה.

nd what does the whole of Israel, that great assembly in which all the Jews join, have to say? Three things:

1. Be patient when you judge—when you make up your mind.

2. Raise up many disciples.

3. Make a fence around the Torah.

1. Why patience? Because that's the hardest thing to learn. Don't make up your mind too quickly. Life is not a baseball game, and you're not an umpire who has to give a decision on the spot. Life is serious, and it goes on for a long time.

2. Why raise up many disciples? Because the great assembly of Israel wants to continue *handing on* its *torah*, the Torah of Moses, and it can only do it to people and through people. It cannot pass on its particular *torah* by writing books. That's the other half of Torah.

3. And make a fence around the Torah. Why? Because good fences make good neighbors? No, because good fences *protect* something. And we want to protect Torah. So we add a bit here and bit there, not too much, but enough to protect what is really important.

MEMORIZING MISHNAH

What helps us memorize our Mishnah is the way it is arranged. Note that we have the same word in the first line and in the last, *Torah*. So this is a Torah-saying. Notice also that each thought is in three parts:

1. Moses received
2. gave to Joshua
3. Joshua to sages.

Or we can see it this way:

Moses received and gave

1. to Joshua

10

2. Joshua to sages
3. sages to prophets.

Then there is a break, which marks the conclusion of the thought:

And the prophets gave it to the men of the great assembly.

The remainder is of course another triplet:

1. Be patient	1. judgment
2. Raise up	2. disciples
3. Make a fence	3. Torah

However you look at it, the little Mishnah we have worked on so hard is easy. To memorize it is a matter of five minutes. But to understand it—that takes a lifetime.

1. What are some of the things we refer to when we use the word Torah?
2. How do you know that Torah is not merely the Five Books of Moses?
3. What is Mishnah? Why is it called Torah shebe'al Peh?
4. How do we know that Mishnah is passed on in a way different from the way in which the written Torah is passed on?
5. Can you sing the first sentence of Abot?
6. Can you explain what the first sentence of Abot says?
7. Why is it important to memorize Mishnah?
8. How is Mishnah memorized? Why is it made into music?
9. Who are the three kinds of people to whom the Oral Torah is given? Why do we need all three kinds of people?
10. What is the message of the great assembly? What are its three parts?

PART TWO

The Common and the Ordinary

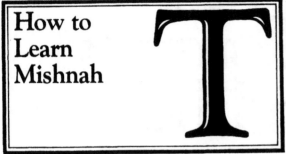

How to Learn Mishnah

The first thing you must know is this: You don't read Mishnah. You *learn* Mishnah.

There is a big difference.

When you read a book, you just go from one idea to the next. You don't have to reflect deeply on one particular sentence or on one paragraph. Everything is open and on the surface. You move right along because there are many books to read, and you can't spend too much time on any of them.

But that is not the same as learning. When you *learn* a book, study it deeply, you don't go fast. You go slowly. You reflect on each problem, on each idea. You build from one idea to the next, adding each bit of knowledge into a building of understanding. You try to grasp the whole.

Mishnah is like math. It has to be learned slowly, with much thought and much reflection. Each sentence has many angles, many approaches. You have to take things apart, line by line and even word by word. But when you do, you see how things really work. When you solve a problem in math properly, you don't just come up with the answer. You have also to show why your answer is true, and , of greatest importance, you have to show *how* you have reached your answer. Mishnah is that way. It is slow and takes thought and analysis.

Second, you must know that Mishnah is not worth knowing unless it is worth knowing for a *reason.* But that is true of anything. If what you are working on is not teaching you something you *want* to know, then work on something else.

If Mishnah is relevant to you, it is because it tells you something you want to know. So in order to study Mishnah, you have to ask *your* questions to Mishnah. You have to find out what it is that Mishnah can tell you about things you want to know.

And that means, third, that you have to ask the right questions to begin with. They have to be "right" in two senses. 1. They must be right for you. And 2. they must be right for Mishnah.

You can't ask Mishnah to tell you how to play football or how to run a

14

race. Those questions are not right for Mishnah. You can't ask Mishnah to tell you how to sacrifice a lamb in the Temple which was destroyed two thousand years ago, or how to decide which ox is at fault when two oxen have gored one another. Those questions are not right for you.

THE RIGHT QUESTIONS

1. The first thing to ask a Mishnah is: What is this Mishnah talking about?

That means, first, do you understand the meaning of *each and every word?* Second, do you understand how the words are put together into sentences? Third, do you understand how the words make it easy to remember what is said? You know how important, in entering into the world of Mishnah, it is to memorize Mishnah. So the first part of the work is to see to it that the language of Mishnah is clear. You have to understand every point and every detail. And then you memorize the Mishnah before you.

2. The second thing to ask a Mishnah is: What is this Mishnah talking about *in its own terms?*

What are the details of the rule, and why are they important? What are the facts that Mishnah knows and thinks you know too? If Mishnah speaks about giving away crops, then be sure you know what that means in real life.

3. The third thing to ask a Mishnah is: What is the human problem about which Mishnah speaks?

What is that human situation which Mishnah knows in *its* terms, and which I know in *my* terms? Can you translate what Mishnah is talking about in its own terms into the world which you know and experience? If you can, then you are a long way into the heart of that Mishnah.

4. The fourth thing to ask a Mishnah is: What are the *choices* people have and make when deciding what to do in this situation which Mishnah is talking about and which I too know about?

How are the problems I know solved by different people? What are the different things people do when faced with that choice which faces Mishnah? And then, how has Mishnah decided things? You have to see that Mishnah chooses between different answers.

5. The fifth thing to ask a Mishnah is: *Why* does Mishnah make the choices it makes? Do these choices make sense? If they make sense, then

why do I think people are wrong who do not do the things the way Mishnah says they should be done? What principle, what ideal, stands behind Mishnah and behind your agreement with Mishnah?

And if they do not make sense, then why do I think the people whose ideas are in Mishnah in this case are wrong? What ideal stands behind Mishnah which I do not accept?

These are only five questions. There are many more you can ask. Once you get inside of a Mishnah, you will realize that you can stay there for a very long time. For Mishnah has been studied for no less than eighteen centuries—1800 years—and that means it has kept people *interested* in what it has to teach for a long time. If that is so, the reason must be that Mishnah keeps peoples' attention. It makes them think.

MISHNAH AND EVERYDAY LIFE

If Mishnah makes you think, and if Mishnah makes you think about the things *it* thinks are important, then Mishnah lives for you. Mishnah therefore will have another forty or fifty or sixty years of life—your life. You want to study Tanakh and teach it to other people who will come after you. And you will want your children and their children to learn Mishnah, just as you do, because Mishnah is the oral half of the Torah, and therefore is one of the two holy books in Judaism.

The important point is that Mishnah has many answers. But we have to find out the correct questions. Mishnah can tell us something only if we learn how to hear what it wants to say. The biggest job you have is asking the right question in the right way. In the earlier, and easier, units which follow, I'll help by asking the question at the outset. Then you'll learn the Mishnah and figure out what it means. Finally, you'll reckon with the answer to the question which *both you and Mishnah are asking.*

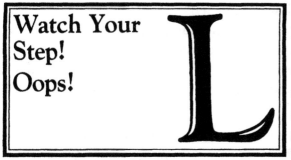

Watch Your Step! Oops!

MISHNAH BABA QAMMA 3:1-4

Living with other people, at home and in school, brings us into conflict. Because we want something, and someone else for the same good reason wants it, we have arguments. Or we do something which makes sense, but someone else doesn't know about it, and there is an accident. I park my bike where it belongs. But, walking in the dark, someone else stumbles over it and cuts an arm or a leg. I walk along and see a dollar bill lying on the ground, and someone else sees it, and we both grab for it at the same time. I find a scarf in the street, and I don't know to whom it belongs. I'd like to keep the scarf. But I'm honest, and I want to try to find the owner. What is my duty?

These are practical questions. As soon as we put them into the language of our own lives, translate them from *their* specific terms of long ago into the equally specific things which happen to *us*, we see that Mishnah is talking about the world in which we live, and it says important things to us.

The first Mishnahs we shall study are long. The reason is not only that they are important, but also that they show us how complicated a question really can be. They spell out a number of different situations. Even though the Mishnahs are long, I'll show you how they're put together and how easy it is to memorize them. Then, if you know them by heart, you can carry them with you back to school and to the sports field, and you can see how the Mishnahs talk about real things which happen to real people. But you'll have to be patient to work through long passages.

The first problem is simple. I leave my bike on the sidewalk in front of my house. Everyone has a right to walk down that sidewalk. Someone stumbles over my bike and falls down and breaks the mirror on the bike. "You broke my mirror!" I exclaim.

"Yeah," he says, "But who told you to leave your bike on the sidewalk? It's your own fault."

Not only is the bike damaged. The person also breaks his glasses. "You should have been more careful," I say.

He says, "I broke my glasses. You pay!"

Mishnah goes over this ground from a number of viewpoints. It gives us several sorts of accidents. But in all, the issue is one and the same. After we've learned the Mishnah, we'll try to restate it in our own terms, and we'll also try to find out the principles of *fairness* which are contained within the Mishnah.

MISHNAH BABA QAMMA 3:1-4

הַמַּנִּיחַ אֶת הַכַּד בִּרְשׁוּת הָרַבִּים, וּבָא אַחֵר וְנִתְקַל בָּה וּשְׁבָרָהּ — פָּטוּר. וְאִם הֻזַּק בָּהּ, בַּעַל הֶחָבִית חַיָּב בְּנִזְקוֹ. נִשְׁבְּרָה כַדּוֹ בִּרְשׁוּת הָרַבִּים, וְהֻחְלַק אֶחָד בַּמַּיִם, אוֹ שֶׁלָּקָה בַּחֲרָסֶיהָ — חַיָּב. רַבִּי יְהוּדָה אוֹמֵר: בְּמִתְכַּוֵּן — חַיָּב; בְּאֵינוֹ מִתְכַּוֵּן — פָּטוּר.

הַשׁוֹפֵךְ מַיִם בִּרְשׁוּת הָרַבִּים, וְהֻזַּק בָּהֶן אַחֵר — חַיָּב בְּנִזְקוֹ. הַמַּצְנִיעַ אֶת הַקּוֹץ, וְאֶת הַזְּכוּכִית, וְהַגּוֹדֵר אֶת גְּדֵרוֹ בַּקּוֹצִים, וְגָדֵר שֶׁנָּפַל לִרְשׁוּת הָרַבִּים, וְהִזִּיקוּ בָּהֶן אֲחֵרִים — חַיָּב בְּנִזְקָן.

הַמּוֹצִיא אֶת תִּבְנוֹ וְאֶת קַשּׁוֹ לִרְשׁוּת הָרַבִּים לִזְבָלִים, וְהֻזַּק בָּהֶן אַחֵר — חַיָּב בְּנִזְקוֹ; וְכָל הַקּוֹדֵם בָּהֶן זָכָה. רַבָּן שִׁמְעוֹן בֶּן גַּמְלִיאֵל אוֹמֵר: כָּל הַמְקַלְקְלִין בִּרְשׁוּת הָרַבִּים, וְהִזִּיקוּ — חַיָּבִין לְשַׁלֵּם; וְכָל הַקּוֹדֵם בָּהֶן זָכָה. הַהוֹפֵךְ אֶת הַגָּלָל בִּרְשׁוּת הָרַבִּים וְהֻזַּק בָּהֶן אַחֵר — חַיָּב בְּנִזְקוֹ. שְׁנֵי קַדָּרִין שֶׁהָיוּ מְהַלְּכִין זֶה אַחַר זֶה, וְנִתְקַל הָרִאשׁוֹן וְנָפַל, וְנִתְקַל הַשֵּׁנִי בָּרִאשׁוֹן — הָרִאשׁוֹן חַיָּב בְּנִזְקֵי הַשֵּׁנִי.

Vocabulary

he who leaves	הַמַּנִּיחַ	stumbles	נִתְקַל
jar	כַּד	broke it	שְׁבָרָהּ
public road	רְשׁוּת הָרַבִּים	free of liability	פָּטוּר
comes	בָּא	is injured	הֻזַּק
another one	אַחֵר	owner	בַּעַל

18

jar	חָבִית		his stubble	קַשּׁוֹ
his injury	נִזְקוֹ		manure	זְבָלִים
slipped	הֶחָלַק		comes first	קוֹדֵם
its sherds	חֲרָסֶיהָ		spoils, damages	מְקַלְקְלִין
liable	חַיָּב		to pay	לְשַׁלֵּם
intend	מִתְכַּוֵּן		turns over	הוֹפֵךְ
pours out	שׁוֹפֵךְ		manure	גָּלָל
water	מַיִם		potters	קַדָּרִין
hides	מַצְנִיעַ		walk along	מְהַלְּכִין
thorn	קוֹץ		one after the other	זֶה אַחַר זֶה
glass	זְכוּכִית			
builds a fence	גּוֹדֵר		fell	נָפַל
fell	נָפַל		second	שֵׁנִי
his straw	תִּבְנוֹ		first	רִאשׁוֹן

How the Mishnah Is Put Together

He who leaves a jar in the public road
1 הַמַּנִּיחַ אֶת הַכַּד בִּרְשׁוּת הָרַבִּים,

and someone else comes along and stumbles on it and breaks it—
וּבָא אַחֵר וְנִתְקַל בָּהּ וּשְׁבָרָהּ —

he is free.
פָּטוּר.

And if he is injured by it, the owner of the jar is liable for his injury.
וְאִם הֻזַּק בָּהּ,
בַּעַל הֶחָבִית חַיָּב בְּנִזְקוֹ.

If his jar is broken in the public way
2 נִשְׁבְּרָה כַדּוֹ בִּרְשׁוּת הָרַבִּים,

19

and someone else slips on the water

or is injured by its sherds

he (the owner) is liable.

R. Judah says, (If he did it) intentionally, he is liable,

(if he did it) not intentionally, he is free (of liability).

וְהֻחְלַק אֶחָד בַּמַּיִם,

אוֹ שֶׁלָּקָה בַחֲרָסֶיהָ —
חַיָּב.

רַבִּי יְהוּדָה אוֹמֵר:
בְּמִתְכַּוֵּן — חַיָּב,
בְּאֵינוֹ מִתְכַּוֵּן — פָּטוּר.

The first Mishnah is put together in a simple way. All it does is state 1. what someone does, 2. what happens because of what someone does, 3. the result: guilty or liable, innocent or free of liability. *Liable* of course means that the person has to pay for the damage which he or she has caused.

In No. 1, therefore, we see in the first clause a simple statement of what someone has done. He set a jar onto the "public way," that is, a path or a sidewalk where anyone has a right to walk. Then what happens? Someone else walks along and stumbles onto the jar, and the jar breaks. That is the second clause. The third clause is simple: the person who broke the jar is free of the obligation to pay for the jar. Why? Because it's not that person's fault. The person who put the jar into the street should have been more careful. There is no way that the person, who had every right to use the public path, is at fault for breaking the jar.

And what happens if the person who stumbled onto the jar and broke it also breaks his arm? Who pays for the doctor? The one who put the jar into the road, naturally.

In No. 2 we have to supply *if* before the beginning of the opening clause. Then the rest is exactly in the model of No. 1. First, we have a statement of what has happened. A person's jar broke in the public way. It had water inside. The water spills onto the road. Then someone else slips on the water. We have yet another description of something which happens. That is to say, the statement of the case is enriched by a second example. But the point, as we shall see, is exactly the same. Now—in this second example—it's not the water that does the damage. When the jar breaks, a sherd hits me in the cheek and cuts me. Does the person who left the jar in the road have to pay for the doctor? He most certainly does.

Judah has a different view. He says: It all depends on what you really *wanted* to have happen. If you intentionally broke the jar and caused the accident, so that someone slipped on the water or got injured by the sherds of the jar, then you are liable. But if you didn't deliberately break the jar and these things happened, you're not liable and owe nothing. What will Judah's opinion be in the first case—No. 1? See if you can figure that out.

How about memorizing? Well, there are two things that help you.

First, you notice that there is a pattern in which *free* alternates with *liable*. In No. 1, we have first *free*, second *liable*. So you have to keep in mind that once you have the one word, you soon are going to have the second. In No. 2, we have *liable*, and then, as the last word, *free*.

The second thing you notice is that you have two clauses to contend with: 1. what someone *does*, and 2. what *happens* to someone else. If you can keep these in mind, it's easy to remember the whole case. Judah's sentence, of course, is simple because you remember *intend/liable, not intend/free*. There could be nothing simpler than that.

MISHNAH BABA QAMMA 3:2

He who pours out water into the public way	1 הַשּׁוֹפֵךְ מַיִם בִּרְשׁוּת הָרַבִּים,
and someone else is injured by it	וְהֻזַּק בָּהֶן אַחֵר —
he (who poured the water) is liable for his injury.	חַיָּב בְּנִזְקוֹ.

2 הַמַּצְנִיעַ אֶת הַקּוֹץ, וְאֶת הַזְּכוּכִית,   He who puts out thorn(s) and glass

וְהַגּוֹדֵר אֶת גְּדֵרוֹ בַּקּוֹצִים,   and he who makes his fence of thorns

וְגָדֵר שֶׁנָּפַל לִרְשׁוּת הָרַבִּים,   and a fence which fell into the public way

וְהֻזְּקוּ בָהֶן אֲחֵרִים —   and other people are hurt by them

חַיָּב בְּנִזְקָן.   he is liable for their injury

e have nothing more than a rerun of the first Mishnah, but the language is slightly different. The case—what someone does—is stated exactly the same: "He who does so and so." The first Mishnah tells us specifically what the injured party has done—he came along and slipped. But in this Mishnah we have a general report. Someone else was injured. It comes down to the same thing. Then we have, "He is liable" but also new language: *for his injury.* That is, the one who poured out the water is liable to pay the doctor's bill for the one who was injured. All this is obvious.

The next part of the Mishnah starts off with a triple-problem. It gives us three separate statements of three different accidents. It's easy to count up three things, you recall. What happens?

1. Somebody put thorns or glass out in the road. It's like putting tacks on the street in front of your house.

Or, 2. somebody makes a hedge out of thorns. It's like people who put glass on top of a fence.

Or, 3. somebody has an ordinary fence, and the fence falls down onto the sidewalk or out onto the road. Then what happens? Exactly what you'd expect. Other people get cut on the glass. Or they drive over the tacks and ruin their tires. Or, walking along normally, they brush up against the thorns and get scratched. Or, when the fence falls down, somebody stumbles into it and gets hurt. What is the result? You know it as well as Mishnah.

MISHNAH BABA QAMMA 3:3

1 He who brings out his straw and stubble to the public way for manure	1 הַמּוֹצִיא אֶת תִּבְנוֹ וְאֶת קַשּׁוֹ לִרְשׁוּת הָרַבִּים לִזְבָלִים,
and someone else was injured by them	וְהֻזַּק בָּהֶן אַחֵר —
he is liable for their injury.	חַיָּב בְּנִזְקוֹ;
And whoever grabs them first can keep them.	וְכָל הַקּוֹדֵם בָּהֶן זָכָה.
Rabban Simeon ben Gamaliel says,	2 רַבָּן שִׁמְעוֹן בֶּן גַּמְלִיאֵל אוֹמֵר:
Whoever do damage in the public way and cause injury	כָּל הַמְקַלְקְלִין בִּרְשׁוּת הָרַבִּים, וְהִזִּיקוּ —
are liable to pay.	חַיָּבִין לְשַׁלֵּם;
And whoever grabs them (things left to mess up public property) can keep them.	וְכָל הַקּוֹדֵם בָּהֶן זָכָה.
He who turns over (heaps up) manure on the public way	3 הַהוֹפֵךְ אֶת הַגָּלָל בִּרְשׁוּת הָרַבִּים,
and someone else is injured by them	וְהֻזַּק בָּהֶן אַחֵר —
is liable for his injury.	חַיָּב בְּנִזְקוֹ.

ow we have still another Mishnah, constructed much like the ones we already know. Someone does something, and someone else is injured on that account. Then what is the rule? At the end we have a clause that tells us what is really new. That is the way No. 1 is built. No. 2 is a return of No. 1. And No. 3 is so familiar in the way it is put together, that we could have put it together ourselves.

In No. 1, somebody puts chopped straw and stubble onto the public road. Why? Because he wants to make them into manure by letting them rot, so that he can use them in his garden. He needs space. So what does he do? He simply takes over part of the public road for his private purposes. Someone stumbles on the rubble and gets hurt. Who is responsible? The answer is obvious. But there's another element here, and that part is not obvious. Can the person say, "Well, since I have to pay the damages, at least I own the things I throw out onto the street?" No, he cannot! Whoever comes along and picks up the straw or the stubble and puts it into his or her own garden has every right to the straw or the stubble. Once you throw stuff onto the road, you have no right to it. Anyone can take it.

There's something curious happening. You're responsible for any damage you cause by throwing something out, but you don't own it.

MISHNAH BABA QAMMA 3:4

Two potters who were going after one another (single-file)	1 שְׁנֵי קַדָּרִין שֶׁהָיוּ מְהַלְּכִין זֶה אַחַר זֶה,
and the first slipped and fell down	וְנִתְקַל הָרִאשׁוֹן וְנָפַל,
and the second slipped on the first	וְנִתְקַל הַשֵּׁנִי בָּרִאשׁוֹן —

the first is liable for the injuries of the second.

הָרִאשׁוֹן חַיָּב בְּנִזְקֵי הַשֵּׁנִי.

This last Mishnah in many ways is the most interesting. There are two potters. Each one carries a pot on his shoulder. The two men are going to deliver the pots to their customers. The streets are narrow, so they have to walk single file. The first potter slips and falls. The second potter slips and falls onto the first. Who pays whom? The first has made *himself* into a public nuisance. The Mishnah points out that he then is responsible for the damage he has caused to the second.

It is built in exactly the same construction which we already know well. First, a statement of what someone does—this time, two people walking single file. Then a statement of what happens, now in two clauses, the first one stumbles and falls down, the second stumbles over the first. Finally, we are told what the rule is: the first one who fell is liable for the injury done to the second.

What is the problem here? Who is responsible for what happens to the second man? The first is responsible. Why? Because he should have yelled to the second, "Hey, watch out! I just fell down." The second man had no warning. He just walked along and stumbled over the first and broke his jar. So the one who stopped short has caused the accident of the other and has to pay for what the second has lost. We don't say, "Well, the second should have been watching where he was going."

WHAT DOES IT MEAN? AND WHAT DOES IT MEAN TO ME?

All these cases say one thing. You are responsible for what you do, and you are responsible for what you do which causes other people injury—even if you do not directly cause the injury. That's the important point. Obviously, if you hit me, you're responsible for what you do to me. But what happens if you don't hit me, but you *cause* me to hurt nonetheless? Mishnah knows exactly what it wants to tell you about that case. In fact, it is so eager to say it that Mishnah says it many different ways. You are responsible not only for what you do directly, but also for what you do indirectly. So you have to be careful to have foresight and to take pains to observe the rules of safety. What you do and what you cause to happen are exactly the same thing and have the same result: You're to blame.

And the reason is obvious. There really is no difference between 1. what I do, 2. what I cause to happen by what I do, and 3. what I cause to happen by what I *don't* do. All of these things have one single result: You made it happen, and you have no claim to say, "Well, I didn't really do it!" Or: "You should have been more careful." Or: "It's *partly* your fault."

If you leave your bike out and someone else accidentally breaks it, that's your fault. You shouldn't have left it out. If someone else is injured by your bike—that's your fault too. If your bike is broken, and the wheel rolls away, and someone else stumbles over the wheel—that's your fault.

If you have a sidewalk in front of your house, and you are out playing with a bubble-pipe, and the bubbles break and spread soapy water on the sidewalk, and your neighbor slips on the water—that's your fault.

If you put out your garbage, and someone slips on it—that's your fault.

If you have a fence with barbs, and someone walks by and tears his coat on the barbed wire fence in front of your house—that's your fault.

If you have a perfectly safe picket fence, but the fence falls down, and you don't pick it up, and someone trips and breaks his ankle on the fence—that's your fault.

If you take out something you want to keep—some fertilizer—and you just leave it out in front of your house, so you don't have to smell it, and someone else comes along and takes the fertilizer and uses it in his garden, too bad for you.

But if someone else falls down into the fertilizer, you have to pay to have his clothes cleaned. You get the worst of both worlds.

And, finally, if you're walking along and fall down, and someone else falls over you, that's your fault too.

Is everything your fault? Yes, it is, *if you don't watch out.* That's what Mishnah is trying to tell you. That's what Mishnah means to you. You must realize that everyone has the same rights to walk in the halls of your school, so you can't leave something sticking out of your locker. Everyone has the same rights to walk down the street in front of your house, so you have to keep your bike off the sidewalk. You have to be careful to *protect* the rights of other people, in those places where everyone has exactly the same rights. You can't ever be careless or sloppy when it comes to places where everyone has a right to come. You can't pretend that what belongs to everyone belongs to you alone.

I call this chapter, "Watch your step!" Who has to watch his or her step? And where do you have to watch your step in particular? Now the answer is clear. The issue is not just who falls down where.

The issue is: What are the responsibilities of people to one another in places in which everyone has the same rights to begin with. That means that there are going to be different sorts of rights and responsibilities in different places and under different circumstances. What you do in your own room, what you put into your own desk or locker—that's another matter.

The issue is not merely fairness. It is what fairness requires in various places and under different circumstances. What you do in your own room, what you put into your own desk or locker—that's another matter.

1. **Why do people who study Mishnah generally start here, with Mishnah Baba Qamma?**

2. **Why do we need so many cases which say the same thing? Why does Rabbi give us five or ten examples of the same point? Wouldn't one be enough?**

3. **What are we supposed to learn from the many cases? Could we have learned that one important point or principle if we had only one case? Could we have learned that one important principle Simeon ben Gamaliel's way—just by saying**

it in so many words? Do you think Rabbi beats around the bush? Or do you think he has an important purpose in giving us so many cases? How would you defend the approach of Simeon ben Gamaliel to the way Mishnah should be said?

4. Why am I responsible for an injury caused by my bike? After all, if I didn't inflict the injury myself, why should I be held liable?

5. Why should I be responsible for the broken mirror? Granted, I have to pay for what I do and for what my broken bike does—but why even for what the sherds of the mirror do?

6. Why can anybody take anything I leave on the street and bring it home? Isn't that stealing?

7. If it's not stealing to take what I leave on the street, then why should I be held responsible if someone trips and falls on something I leave there? If it's not mine, if anyone can have it, then why is it mine when it comes to paying for injuries caused by it?

8. Judah thinks much depends on whether you mean it or not. If you don't mean to cause damage, then you're not really responsible. Why does everyone else disagree with Judah? What can you say in behalf of Judah's point?

9. Why am I responsible if I accidentally fall down and someone trips on me? After all, I didn't fall down purposely. I had an accident. The other guy had an accident too. If no one pays me, why should I pay him? Do you think Judah agrees with this rule?

10. If you had to write this Mishnah, would you be able to give examples of each and every case which Mishnah has given us? What are the separate and distinct points Mishnah wants to make, and how would we make the same points in our own way and in the cases of our own day?

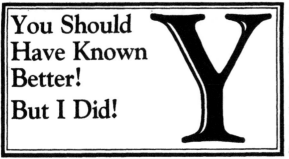

You Should Have Known Better! But I Did!

MISHNAH BABA QAMMA 6:1-3

You clearly bear the blame for many things. You are responsible not only for your actions, but also for situations which you cause. But is there no limit to the matter? Isn't there any way that you can say, "I did what I was supposed to do. What happened is an accident, but I didn't *make* it happen. In fact, I did what I could to stop it from happening. So whoever is at fault—I'm not."

There are limits. You are responsible to do your job. But if you have done your job, have taken pains to prevent an accident and not to cause one, then, if something does happen, you're not to blame. No one is.

That's the point of the next Mishnah, another long one. Mishnah has much to say about many things. It simply can't say everything it wants to tell us in just one case or in just a few words. Because the issue at hand—*responsibility for what you do*—is complicated. You are responsible for what you do, but sometimes you've done all you can do, and that means that, after that point, what happens just isn't your fault. So responsibility is limited. There are events you cause. There are situations you can try to prevent. And there are things which just happen, despite the best you can do to stop them.

As you know, Mishnah doesn't like generalities. It loves specific cases and problems. And the way in which Mishnah tells us about the limits of our responsibilities is through one specific case: what a person's dog does. Mishnah, of course, is going to talk about what it knows, so it will tell us about sheep and cows and damage they do to other people's gardens and houses. You have a dog, and the problem is the same. The dog is gentle and kind, especially when the dog is with you. But sometimes the dog breaks out and joins other dogs and becomes part of a pack of wild dogs. And it does a lot of damage. Are you responsible? Why? When are you *not* responsible? In other words, the issue of responsibility is spelled out through the actions of things that you own, but which you cannot always control. Now let's come to our Mishnah.

MISHNAH BABA QAMMA 6:1-3

הַכּוֹנֵס צֹאן לַדִּיר וְנָעַל בִּפְנֵיהָ כָּרָאוּי, וְיָצְאָה וְהִזִּיקָה —
פָּטוּר. לֹא נָעַל בִּפְנֵיהָ כָּרָאוּי, וְיָצְאָה וְהִזִּיקָה — חַיָּב. נִפְרְצָה
בַּלַּיְלָה אוֹ שֶׁפְּרָצוּהָ לִסְטִים, וְיָצְאָה וְהִזִּיקָה — פָּטוּר. הוֹצִיאוּהָ
לִסְטִים, הַלִּסְטִים חַיָּבִים.   הִנִּיחָהּ בַּחַמָּה, אוֹ שֶׁמְּסָרָהּ לְחֵרֵשׁ,
שׁוֹטֶה וְקָטָן, וְיָצְאָה וְהִזִּיקָה — חַיָּב. מְסָרָהּ לְרוֹעֶה, נִכְנַס הָרוֹעֶה
תַּחְתָּיו. נָפְלָה לַגַּנָּה וְנֶהֱנֵית, מְשַׁלֶּמֶת מַה שֶׁנֶּהֱנֵית. יָרְדָה כְּדַרְכָּהּ
וְהִזִּיקָה, מְשַׁלֶּמֶת מַה שֶׁהִזִּיקָה. כֵּיצַד מְשַׁלֶּמֶת מַה שֶׁהִזִּיקָה?
שָׁמִין בֵּית סְאָה בְּאוֹתָהּ שָׂדֶה, כַּמָּה הָיְתָה יָפָה וְכַמָּה הִיא יָפָה?
רַבִּי שִׁמְעוֹן אוֹמֵר: אָכְלָה פֵּרוֹת גְּמוּרִים, מְשַׁלֶּמֶת פֵּרוֹת גְּמוּרִים;
אִם סְאָה סְאָה, אִם סָאתַיִם סָאתַיִם.   הַמַּגְדִּישׁ בְּתוֹךְ שָׂדֶה
שֶׁלַּחֲבֵרוֹ שֶׁלֹּא בִרְשׁוּת, וַאֲכָלָתַן בְּהֶמְתּוֹ שֶׁלְּבַעַל הַשָּׂדֶה — פָּטוּר;
וְאִם הֻזְּקָה בָּהֶן, בַּעַל הַגָּדִישׁ חַיָּב; וְאִם הִגְדִּישׁ בִּרְשׁוּת, בַּעַל
הַשָּׂדֶה חַיָּב.

Vocabulary

he who brings in	הַכּוֹנֵס	sun	חַמָּה
flock	צֹאן	deaf-mute	חֵרֵשׁ
to a fold	לַדִּיר	person not in control of his senses	שׁוֹטֶה
locked	נָעַל		
before it (the flock)	בִּפְנֵיהָ	minor, someone not of age	קָטָן
properly	כָּרָאוּי		
went out	יָצְאָה	shepherd	רוֹעֶה
it was broken down	נִפְרְצָה	went in	נִכְנַס
at night	בַּלַּיְלָה	in his place, instead of him	תַּחְתָּיו
robbers	לִסְטִים		
he left it	הִנִּיחָהּ	fell	נָפְלָה

30

garden, field of vegetables	גִּנָּה	worth	יָפָה
		consumed	אָכְלָה
enjoyed, derived benefit from	נֶהֱנֵית	complete, ripe	גְּמוּרִים
		he who stacks	הַמַּגְדִּישׁ
pays	מְשַׁלֶּמֶת	inside	בְּתוֹךְ
in the usual way	כְּדַרְכָּהּ	of his fellow	שֶׁלַּחֲבֵרוֹ
how	כֵּיצַד		
they estimate	שָׁמִין	his cow	בְּהֶמְתּוֹ
an area sown by a seah of seeds	בֵּית סְאָה	owner of the field	בַּעַל הַשָּׂדֶה
field	שָׂדֶה		
how much	כַּמָּה		

How the Mishnah Is Put Together

He who brings (his) flock into a fold and locked it in properly	1 הַכּוֹנֵס צֹאן לַדִּיר וְנָעַל בְּפָנֶיהָ כָּרָאוּי,
and it went out and did damage	וְיָצְאָה וְהִזִּיקָה —
he is free (of liability)	פָּטוּר.
(If) he did not lock it in properly	לֹא נָעַל בְּפָנֶיהָ כָּרָאוּי,
and it (the flock) went out and did damage	וְיָצְאָה וְהִזִּיקָה —
he is liable (for damage done by the flock)	חַיָּב.
(If) the fold was broken down at night	2 נִפְרְצָה בַּלַּיְלָה

or robbers broke it down	אוֹ שֶׁפְּרָצוּהָ לִסְטִים,
and it (the flock) got out and did damage	וְיָצְאָה וְהִזִּיקָה —
he is free (of liability)	פָּטוּר.
(If) the robbers took it (the flock) out (of the fold)	3 הוֹצִיאוּהָ לִסְטִים,
the robbers are liable (for damage done by the flock)	הַלִּסְטִים חַיָּבִים.

ur Mishnah is built on a familiar model. It simply tells us 1. what someone does, 2. what happens on that account, and 3. the decision we make. 1. Some one does something. 2. Something happens. 3. The person who did it is either liable or free of liability.

No. 1 is a perfect set of three matching sentences. What do I do? I have a flock of sheep. I put the flock into its fold. I lock the gate. I do it just the way I should. But the flock gets out and then goes into someone's field and eats up the crop. Am I liable? No, I am not liable to pay for the crop. Why not? Because I did everything I could have done. This is an accident. But No. 1 goes on, let's now reverse the matter. I lock up the flock, but I don't do it right. The flock goes out and eats up someone else's crops. Of course I'm liable. I could have prevented the damage. Every word is matched, line by line, because the two events are mirror images of one another. All this is simple.

You can easily translate it into the world you know. You have a dog. It's a watch dog. You tie it up at night. The knot is tight, and the rope is thick. Everything you could do, you have done. But somehow the dog gets free and knocks over someone's garbage pail. Do you have to go and pick up the garbage? No, you don't have to (though, if you're nice, you will anyhow). But what happens if you tie up the dog, but you use a shoestring. That's not going to hold the dog. And it doesn't. The dog gets free and bites your neighbor. Who do you think pays?

No. 2 continues our case. You lock up the sheep. But the wall falls down at night. Or some thieves come and knock it down. The sheep get out and eat up your neighbor's corn. Who pays? Not you. You did what you're supposed to. There was an accident, and the fence, which you left standing, fell down. Or someone else knocked it down. That isn't your fault. This, of course, is easy enough to translate into today's terms.

What happened is that you tied up your dog with a good rope. But as it happens, during the night there was a thunder storm, and the rope got wet and somehow snapped. Or someone else came along and untied the dog. The dog bit your neighbor. You don't have to pay.

At the end we have something obvious. A thief came and untied the flock—or your dog—and then the flock ate up your neighbor's corn—or the dog bit your neighbor—but then the thief is caught! Who pays? Well, obviously, the thief is responsible, and, if he's got the money, he pays for the damages he has caused.

There's nothing surprising in this rule except for its basic point: there are *limits* to responsibility. This is the opposite side of the lesson we learned just now. You must take responsibility for yourself and what you own. But if you do what you're supposed to do, then that fact is important and taken into account.

MISHNAH BABA QAMMA 6:2

(If) he left it in the sun	1 הִנִּיחָהּ בַּחַמָּה,
or gave it over to a deaf-mute, someone not in command of his senses, or a minor	אוֹ שֶׁמְּסָרָהּ לְחֵרֵשׁ, שׁוֹטֶה וְקָטָן,
and it got out and did damage	וְיָצְאָה וְהִזִּיקָה —
he is liable (for damage caused by the flock)	חַיָּב.

(If) he gave it over to a shepherd	2 מְסָרָהּ לָרוֹעֶה,
the shepherd stands in his (the owner's) place	נִכְנַס הָרוֹעֶה תַּחְתָּיו.
(If) it fell into a garden and derived benefit	3 נָפְלָה לַגִּנָּה וְנֶהֱנֵית,
it (the flock, meaning the owner) pays for what it enjoyed	מְשַׁלֶּמֶת מַה שֶׁנֶּהֱנֵית.
(If) it went down in its usual way and did damage	4 יָרְדָה כְדַרְכָּהּ וְהִזִּיקָה,
it pays for what it damaged	מְשַׁלֶּמֶת מַה שֶׁהִזִּיקָה.
How does it pay for what it damaged?	5 כֵּיצַד מְשַׁלֶּמֶת מַה שֶׁהִזִּיקָה?
They reckon a *seah*'s space of ground in that field	שָׁמִין בֵּית סְאָה בְּאוֹתָהּ שָׂדֶה,
what it was worth and how much it (now) is worth (and the man pays the difference).	כַּמָּה הָיְתָה יָפָה וְכַמָּה הִיא יָפָה?
Rabbi Simeon says, (If) it ate fully grown produce, it pays the cost of fully grown produce.	רַבִּי שִׁמְעוֹן אוֹמֵר: אָכְלָה פֵּרוֹת גְּמוּרִים, מְשַׁלֶּמֶת פֵּרוֹת גְּמוּרִים;
(If the flock destroyed) one *seah*, (the man must repay) one *seah*, (and) if (the flock destroyed) two *seahs*, (the man must repay) two *seahs*.	אִם סְאָה סְאָה, אִם סָאתַיִם סָאתַיִם.

ishnah wants to make its point again: What you do to carry out your responsibilities determines whether you are responsible. We take the flock and lock it up. But we leave the sheep in the sun, and they go wild. They jump over the fence. Or we lock the sheep up, but we appoint as guard someone who can't be relied upon. The sheep escape and damage property. Who pays? You do.

Let's go back to your dog. You tie it up. But you leave the dog without water, and the dog begins to bark. Finally, with a great effort, the dog pulls at its rope and breaks it. Now, you did the right thing, but you didn't do it in the right way. Who pays? You do.

The next rule is the opposite of this one. It's worded in a simple way. If you put the sheep in the hands of a reliable shepherd, and you pay the shepherd a fee, you most certainly have done the right thing. You're not responsible any more for damage the sheep may do. The shepherd knows his business, and he takes responsibility. There's nothing surprising here. The important thing Mishnah wants to say is that when you don't use the right kind of guard, you're responsible, but when you do, you're not responsible because the guard takes responsibility. You did your job.

Then we go on to No. 3, to a new question. We know that under certain conditions you're responsible and have to pay damages. What do you have to pay?

Here we have two rules, Nos. 3 and 4. No. 3 says that the sheep got into a garden and chewed up some plants. This was an accident. You couldn't have known that the flock would happen to cut through the garden. What do you have to pay? You pay what you gained: the plants that the sheep ate. But do you have to pay for the damage to the fence or to other plants which the sheep damaged? No, you only pay for what your sheep actually ate. That, after all, is food, and you benefit from the sheep eating.

But what happens if it is not really an accident. That is, the sheep deliberately go into your neighbor's garden and damage the fence, walk over plants and eat up some of the plants. What do you pay for now? Since this was deliberate and not accidental, you pay for the whole thing: the fence, the plants which were damaged, and, of course, also for the plants which were eaten. You can easily translate this into the damage done by your dog.

No. 5 is a bit technical, but there's no reason that we can't figure it out. How do you pay for the damage your sheep have caused in No. 4? There are two rules. The first is that you reckon the total value of the damage. How? You figure out the value of the field before the sheep broke in, and the value after the sheep have damaged the field. You pay the difference. But you don't have to reckon the cost of the actual row of turnips or beets which the sheep have eaten. There is a real difference. If you pay for each and every turnip, it can be expensive. But if you figure out what you owe in terms of the whole value of the field before, and after, it was ruined, it comes to somewhat less money. Simeon doesn't agree. He says that you should pay for what you did. The sheep ate ripe fruit, so you pay for ripe fruit—you pay for exactly what you've eaten. That comes to more money, of course. The difference of opinion is interesting. It shows that even when you know you have to pay, there still are different ideas of how to figure out just how much.

MISHNAH BABA QAMMA 6:3

He who stacks sheaves in the field of his friend without permission	1 הַמַּגְדִּישׁ בְּתוֹךְ שָׂדֶה שֶׁלַּחֲבֵרוֹ שֶׁלֹּא בִרְשׁוּת,
and the cow of the owner of the field ate them up	וַאֲכָלָתַן בְּהֶמְתּוֹ שֶׁלְבַעַל הַשָּׂדֶה —
(the owner of the field) is free (of liability).	פָּטוּר;
And if it (the cattle belonging to owner of the field) was injured by it (the sheaves of grain)	2 וְאִם הֻזְּקָה בָהֶן,
the owner of the sheaves of grain is liable.	בַּעַל הַגָּדִישׁ חַיָּב;

But if he stacked sheaves
with permission, the owner
of the field is liable.

3 וְאִם הִגְדִּישׁ בִּרְשׁוּת,
בַּעַל הַשָּׂדֶה חַיָּב.

he third case has no surprises. It's like the first. It states something someone does, then it tells about something that happens on that account, and, finally, it states the rule. We go on to No. 2 to add another important point, this time with an *if*, and then to No. 3, which is an exact match to No. 2.

The rule is simple. It's the *case* which is important. I have a load of corn-sheaves. I have to store them somewhere. I store them on my neighbor's property. I don't ask permission. Maybe he's on a trip, and I can't ask. I assume he won't mind, and he doesn't—because sometimes he uses a corner of my land too. But what happens? His cow comes along and eats my sheaves of corn. Who pays? Not the owner of the cow, who also is the owner of the land. Why not? Because he never gave me permission to keep my sheaves of corn there, and he, therefore, is not responsible for anything that happens to them.

If your father and mother park their car in a parking lot and don't get permission or pay a fee, and someone drives along and smashes up their car, the owner of the parking lot is not responsible, because no one ever asked him to watch out for the car. Or, if a robber comes and breaks into the car, whose fault is it? It's not the fault of the parking lot owner. He never said he'd guard your car, and you didn't even ask him to.

No. 2 raises the obvious question: But what happens if you pile up your grain, and the owner of the field—and remember, you never asked him for permission to pile up your grain in his field—walks along and stumbles into the sheaves of corn and falls down and breaks his arm? What happens? Pay up, friend. It's your fault. The same goes for the injury to his cattle.

And, No. 3 finishes up by saying what we already know: *If the owner of the field gives permission for you to pile up your corn in his field, and then his cow eats your corn, who pays?* He does, because he gave permission and therefore takes responsibility. No. 3 really continues No. 1. No. 2 has interrupted the flow of thought. For No. 1 asks about doing something *without* permission, and No. 3 asks about doing something *with* permission, and the two are exact matches for one another. No. 2 breaks in to tell us something obvious but also important. It is an "interpolation"—something someone throws into the construction, breaking it up, but also building it up.

WHAT DOES IT MEAN TO ME?

In the opening Mishnah of this division, we learn that we take responsibility for what we do. And in this, the matching Mishnah, we learn that when we do carry out our responsibility, there are limits to what can be blamed on us. These are two important ideas. One without the other would mislead us.

What if I knew only the first of the two Mishnahs? Then I should take to heart the lesson that I have to be careful about how I take care of my things. I have to watch out, in particular, for what I do when I am in a place where other people have rights too. But for all I know, that means, I'm always going to be blamed for whatever happens.

What if I knew only the second of the two Mishnahs? Then I'd know that once I do my duty, I'm really not to blame at all. That is without regard to where I am or to the rights of others in the same place.

So the two Mishnahs complete one another. The first one tells me that, when I don't do my duty, I'm going to take the blame. But this is especially so when I am in a place where anyone has a right to be. But, the second Mishnah says, when I am in my own home, and I take care of my property in the right way, and then something happens, I'm not to blame.

The second Mishnah tells me that I'm responsible for what I do, but not for what other people do to my property. But this is limited, too, by the first Mishnah, which says that as far as public property is concerned, I have to take much more responsibility than I would imagine. If I fall down and someone falls on me—I'm responsible.

You're beginning to realize that a few simple rules of life—"be nice to

38

other people," "take care not to hurt them either by what you do or what you don't do"—are not enough. Life is too complicated to be taken care of by a few simple rules. There are many rules which you're going to need to take account of all the claims people can make against one another. There's a little bit of right on every side. There are possibilities which you can control, and situations that you can't stop. Some things that you can't stop will still be your fault. Some that you can stop may not be your fault. It's just not easy to make a Mishnah. But when you have a Mishnah, look what you've got! See what you've gained. You've learned something which few people know but everyone needs to learn.

You've learned how to think through what you are supposed to do, and you've learned how to figure out what your duties are. And nothing is more important than that. You live with other people, in *society*, and the most important thing you have to find out—and continually try to find out—is just *how* to do so: *What do you owe other people? And what do you owe yourself?*

1. Why is it important to set limits on things for which you are responsible? What would be the alternative?
2. Why doesn't Mishnah like generalities? Why does it prefer to talk about specific cases? Does it make it harder for us to learn Mishnah? In what ways? But in what ways does it make it easier for us to learn Mishnah?
3. Is it fair to talk about a dog instead of the sheep or cows about which Mishnah speaks?
4. Can you see a pattern in the way in which Mishnah lays out its cases? Can you outline that pattern of wording? If you can, are you now able to make up your own case, using the example of your dog, in the model of Mishnah's?
5. Why is closing the gate before the flock of sheep parallel to tying up your dog? But is there a difference between a sheep and a dog?
6. Why are you not responsible if the wall falls down? Why are you not responsible if a thief opens the gate before the sheep?
7. Why is it important to put your sheep in the hands of someone who can take responsibility? Why is the shepherd liable for the damage the sheep cause? Why is someone not in control of himself not responsible? Why are you responsible if you give the sheep to someone who can't do the job?
8. Why do we distinguish the damages you have to pay if your sheep accidentally go into someone else's field, or if there is some accident which leads them there, from damages which you have to pay if your sheep go into the field of the other person in a perfectly routine and normal way? What difference is there between unusual and usual things?
9. Why is it important to get the permission of the owner of the field before you pile up your corn there? Why doesn't the owner have to pay if his cow eats corn you pile up without his permission? Why do you have to pay if you pile up your corn without permission and the owner happens to stumble into it and break his leg?

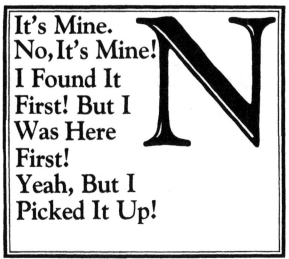

It's Mine.
No, It's Mine!
I Found It
First! But I
Was Here
First!
Yeah, But I
Picked It Up!

MISHNAH BABA MEṢI 'A' 1:3-4

ow let's come closer to home. Not everyone has a dog. And not every dog breaks its rope and then bites a neighbor. But at some time or other, you must have had an argument with someone else over something you found in the street.

You and your friend are walking down the street. You have your eyes on the ground, and your friend is looking up in the air. Suddenly you see a quarter. Your friend is nearer to it. You say, "Hey, look down and pick up that quarter." He does. But then he puts it into his pocket. You are angry.

"I saw it first," you say.

"Yeah," he says, "But I picked it up, and it's in my pocket."

Who has a right to the quarter?

You'd better have an answer to that question. Because if you don't you're going to be angry with your friend—who will keep the quarter. Or he's going to be angry with you—when you take it away from him. Now life can't go on this way. You should have some notion of what is fair, so that every time you and your friend are walking together and find something, you don't end your friendship on the spot. *Fair is fair*—but what's fair?

This sort of thing happens every day. If you don't have Mishnah on your mind, you're going to have fights and arguments, and there's going to be ill-will between you and other people. But if you and your friends do have Mishnah on your minds, then you all have somewhere to turn, a fair and impartial rule that applies and can help you settle your arguments.

It's natural to have arguments and to want things that other people want. But it's not good for arguments never to come to an end, and it's not healthy for any group of friends not to have some common and shared sense of what is right and fair. And that's what Mishnah gives you.

This time we're going to learn only two Mishnahs, which are a bit easier than the ones which you've just figured out. You've been working hard, and it's time to take it a bit easier.

MISHNAH BABA MEṢI'A' 1:3-4

הָיָה רוֹכֵב עַל גַּבֵּי בְהֵמָה וְרָאָה אֶת הַמְּצִיאָה, וְאָמַר לַחֲבֵרוֹ: ׳תְּנֶה לִי׳, נְטָלָה וְאָמַר: ׳אֲנִי זָכִיתִי בָהּ׳ — זָכָה בָהּ. אִם מִשֶּׁנְּתָנָהּ לוֹ אָמַר: ׳אֲנִי זָכִיתִי בָהּ תְּחִלָּה׳ — לֹא אָמַר כְּלוּם. רָאָה אֶת הַמְּצִיאָה וְנָפַל עָלֶיהָ, וּבָא אַחֵר וְהֶחֱזִיק בָּהּ — זֶה שֶׁהֶחֱזִיק בָּהּ זָכָה בָהּ. רָאָה אוֹתָן רָצִין אַחַר מְצִיאָה: אַחַר צְבִי שָׁבוּר, אַחַר גּוֹזָלוֹת שֶׁלֹּא פָּרְחוּ, וְאָמַר: ׳זָכְתָה לִי שָׂדִי׳ — זָכְתָה לוֹ. הָיָה צְבִי רָץ כְּדַרְכּוֹ, אוֹ שֶׁהָיוּ גוֹזָלוֹת מַפְרִיחִין, וְאָמַר: ׳זָכְתָה לִי שָׂדִי׳ — לֹא אָמַר כְּלוּם.

Vocabulary

was	הָיָה	I	אֲנִי
riding	רוֹכֵב	acquired possession	זָכִיתִי
on	עַל	of it	בָהּ
top of	גַּבֵּי	if	אִם
cow	בְהֵמָה	after he gave it	מִשֶּׁנְּתָנָהּ
saw	רָאָה	to him	לוֹ
lost property	מְצִיאָה	first	תְּחִלָּה
said	אָמַר	not	לֹא
his friend	חֲבֵרוֹ	nothing	כְּלוּם
give it	תְּנֶה	and he fell	וְנָפַל
to me	לִי	on it	עָלֶיהָ
he took it	נְטָלָה	he came	בָּא

someone else	אַחֵר	pigeons	גוֹזָלוֹת
grabbed, seized	הֶחֱזִיק	flying	פָּרְחוּ
them	אוֹתָן	my field	שָׂדִי
running	רָצִין	ran	רָץ
gazelle	צְבִי	normally	כְּדַרְכּוֹ
lame	שָׁבוּר	flying	מַפְרִיחִין

How the Mishnah Is Put Together

(If) he was riding on a cow and saw lost property	1 הָיָה רוֹכֵב עַל גַּבֵּי בְהֵמָה וְרָאָה אֶת הַמְּצִיאָה,
and he said to his friend, "Give it to me"	וְאָמַר לַחֲבֵרוֹ: 'תְּנֶהָ לִי';
(and the other) took it and said, "I acquired possession of it first"	נְטָלָהּ וְאָמַר: 'אֲנִי זָכִיתִי בָהּ' —
he (the other) has acquired possession of it.	זָכָה בָהּ.
If after he gave it to him, he said, "I acquired possession of it first"	2 אִם מִשֶּׁנְּתָנָהּ לוֹ אָמַר: 'אֲנִי זָכִיתִי בָהּ תְּחִלָּה' —
he has said nothing.	לֹא אָמַר כְּלוּם.

The first thing you notice is that you've seen this kind of construction before. We have a story of something that happened. But now it is a kind of conversation. Someone was going somewhere and then— *he said.* So, No. 1 tells us someone was riding along on a beast, and he saw lost property. Then he said to his friend, who was walking alongside, "Give it to me." And the friend picked it up and said, "I take it for myself." Then at the end: He gets to keep it. He has acquired possession for himself. So at the crucial moment, the matter depends on what someone *says*, and whether what he says is valid.

That is clear in No. 2. If the friend gave it to the man riding on the beast but then said, "Still, I took it for myself first," the friend has said nothing.

The matter of what someone says is introduced at every turning point in the story. And the purpose of the story is to tell us whether or not what someone says is valid. If it is, then the person gets to keep the lost property. And if not, the person doesn't.

What's the point of the conflict? It has to do with two things, 1. *doing* something, and 2. *saying* something. One fellow is on the donkey. He spots the lost property. He says to his friend, "Hand it up to me." Now, if the friend doesn't hand it up but just keeps it for himself, what claim has the man on the donkey? None at all. It never *was* his property. It isn't his property now. And it never will be. Because all that happened is that he saw it. And he asked for it. The one who is walking along picks it up and keeps it. That's his right. Fair is fair. Finders keepers.

But what happens if the one walking along does pick up the lost property and hands it over to the man on the donkey? Then the situation changes. Who has the property? The man on the donkey. Does anything the other man say change that fact? Of course not! Losers weepers.

That's this part of the story. Its meaning is obvious. If something is lying there, free for the asking, then the person who picks it up first has the right to keep it. Nothing anyone else says comes into play.

MISHNAH BABA MEṢI'A' 1:4

1   רָאָה אֶת הַמְּצִיאָה וְנָפַל עָלֶיהָ,
(If) he saw the lost property and fell on it

וּבָא אַחֵר וְהֶחֱזִיק בָּהּ —
and someone else came along. and seized it

זֶה שֶׁהֶחֱזִיק בָּהּ זָכָה בָּהּ.
this one who seized it has acquired possession of it.

2   רָאָה אוֹתָן רָצִין אַחַר מְצִיאָה:
(If) he saw them running after lost property

אַחַר צְבִי שָׁבוּר,
after a lame gazelle

אַחַר גּוֹזָלוֹת שֶׁלֹּא פֵרְחוּ,
after pigeons which were not flying

וְאָמַר: 'זָכְתָה לִי שָׂדִי' —
and said, "My field has acquired possession for me,"

זָכְתָה לוֹ.
it (the field) has acquired possession for him.

3   הָיָה צְבִי רָץ כְּדַרְכּוֹ,
(If) it was a gazelle running normally

אוֹ שֶׁהָיוּ גוֹזָלוֹת מַפְרִיחִין,
or pigeons flying

וְאָמַר: 'זָכְתָה לִי שָׂדִי' —
and he said, "My field has acquired possession for me,"

לֹא אָמַר כְּלוּם.
he has said nothing whatsoever.

45

his rich Mishnah completes the one we just learned, and it also gives us a new problem.

The first part, No. 1, involves a man walking along. He sees lost property. He doesn't say a thing. He falls on it, so as to take it for himself. Then someone else comes along and grabs it away. The law is that the one who grabs it away gets to keep it. We notice once more that the Mishnah sets up a situation—someone saw and did something—and then says what happens in that situation, and at the end gives its rule. This is fairly easy to remember.

What's the point now? Why does the Mishnah say that the one who falls on the property loses it to the one who grabs it *and holds on to it?* Is it because might makes right? Hardly. The reason is simple. By falling on the lost property—which is in the public way—the man has done nothing whatsoever. He has not taken the property and made it his own. The one who afterward comes and grabs it does indeed do something which makes the property his own. This point becomes clearer in the next part of the Mishnah.

Let's begin our look into No. 2 by noticing that we have too many stories at the outset—three in all. One would have been sufficient to make the point.

A man sees people running. Where do you think they are running? It is in the man's own field, on his own property. They're running to get lost property. Or they're running after a lame gazelle. Or they're running after pigeons which cannot fly. They hope to catch the gazelle or the pigeons and take them home, slaughter them properly and eat them.

Then comes what is, by now, expected: What the man actually does. He doesn't do a thing. He *says* something. What he says is this: "Let my field take possession for me."

That is, the lost property, or the animal, or the pigeon, is in the man's own property. All he does, therefore, is to claim in his own right what already is on his own land. That's fair enough. When he says so, then he becomes the rightful owner of the property.

On the other hand, No. 3 adds, if the gazelle was running along, or the pigeons were flying and just happened to light on his field, does the man have a right to the animal or bird? Hardly. Why not? Because these things are not necessarily going to stay where they are now. They are not within the man's right. The field is just one that they're crossing. And they're moving along rapidly, under their own power. Merely by saying, "Let my field take them for me," the man says nothing at all. If the man himself were to run after the gazelle or the pigeon, he could never catch it. So why should his field do what he himself can't do?

This brings us back to No. 1. Why doesn't the man who falls on the lost property acquire it? Because he's not on his *own* land. He really hasn't done anything to make the lost property his own. The one who comes along and takes it up in his hand has taken possession. He has made the lost property his own. Since the lost property is in the yard of neither one, the man who takes it up and holds on to it keeps it.

The real point is simple. What's lost is lost—and no one owns it. So if you want to make yourself the rightful owner, you have to do something concrete and specific to turn the lost property into something no longer lost. It is made into something in your own possession, and, in fact, is made yours. What you have to do is spelled out in the cases before us.

On the one hand, if you say to someone else, "Give me that thing," and the person ignores what you say and takes it for himself, it's his, not yours. You haven't *done* anything.

On the other hand, if you say to him, "Give me that thing," and he gives it to you, and only *then* does he say to you, "But I had it first"—it's yours, not his. Why? Because you have it and have made it your own.

Words don't help you in the first case, and they don't help your friend in the second case.

And then there's that other matter—just stepping on a penny on the ground and thinking that it's yours. Someone else comes and pushes your foot and takes the penny and puts it into his pocket. Mishnah says it's his, not yours. So there is more than just the matter of words. There's the matter of deeds, indeed, a specific action. Merely stepping on the penny ("falling on the lost property") doesn't do it. Why not? Because you haven't bent down and picked up the penny and put it into your pocket.

But, our second Mishnah goes on, what happens if you're on your own property? Mishnah doesn't have to say that if you step on a penny in your own yard, that makes it yours. After all, it's your yard. The penny probably came from your pocket to begin with. Mishnah doesn't waste our time by telling us what we already know.

Instead it sets up an interesting problem. If something is moving along but is bound to end up in your yard, and you say, "Let my yard take possession of it for me"—that's enough. This is not quite lost property, but it is ownerless property. You make yourself the owner by using your yard to take over what is ownerless and holding on to it.

However, if something is not going to end up in your yard but is just passing through or flying by, then all the words in the world won't help you. After all, the thing is just not going to stop moving when it enters your gate.

WHAT DOES IT MEAN TO ME?

This practical Mishnah is meaningful because it talks about things that happen every day. So you must be thinking, here at last is a Mishnah which I don't have to translate into my everyday life. It already is in the words which I speak every day and talks about things I see and know about at home.

But that really isn't true. Because for Mishnah to talk about things near at hand, other people have to be listening to it just as much as you listen to it. And that isn't likely to happen. Most people don't know what you now know, that is what Mishnah says about keeping a lost penny. If you claim, "according to Mishnah, it's mine," someone might just haul off and knock your block off.

And what Mishnah really wants to tell you—whether it's talking about sheep a thousand years ago or a penny you found this morning—is what's fair and *how* you should do what's fair. It can't tell you how to make other people do what's fair. The world doesn't listen to our Mishnah. Mishnah can only tell you how to think about what's fair, but you have to try to make the world a fair place in which to live.

That doesn't mean Mishnah isn't relevant to you. It certainly is. Because Mishnah is telling you how to look at a problem and how to take it apart, how to unpack it and then put it back together again. That's valuable knowledge. What it wants you to know about lost property is that it's *really lost: it really doesn't belong to anyone.* And if you want to make it belong to someone, you have to do something about it. Just saying something doesn't change the fact that the property is lost. You haven't done anything to make it less lost. All you've done is to say that you'd like it.

Mishnah says that you have to put your hand down and pick up that penny if you can. Or you have to see to it that what comes into your yard remains there and actually belongs to you. That effort is what is takes to turn lost property into your property.

Of course we can't leave matters here. After all, there's another side to lost and found—which is, *found.* Who really owns something? When do you find something and get to keep it, and when do you find something and have to look around to see who might own it? That's another question entirely, and one that Mishnah will now tell us how to solve.

1. **Why do you think it's fair to hold on to something merely because you saw it first? Why do you become angry with your friend who picks up the quarter and puts it into his pocket? Is there some right on your side too? But if there is, then why does Mishnah still award the quarter to your friend?**

2. **People who study our Mishnah say that the purpose of Mishnah is to prevent squabbling. How does Mishnah keep you from having a big fight with your friend over that quarter he has put into his pocket?**

3. **If you were putting Mishnah into language anyone today would understand, how would you state the case, or the story, of the first Mishnah? What would be a situation similar to the one about the man riding on the donkey?**

4. **Why doesn't the friend get to keep the lost property once he hands it over to you? Doesn't he have any rights to it? What claim can he make? Why, nonetheless, does Mishnah still award the lost property to the person who now has it?**

5. **Mishnah speaks of a limping gazelle or pigeons which can't fly. Can you think of any thing which would be like these**

things, which might land in your yard for you to claim and take possession of? Why is it so important that your yard "take possession" for you? And why do you have to say, "Let my backyard take possession"? Why doesn't it happen automatically?

6. Why does the man who just steps on a penny not thereby own the penny? Why does Mishnah say that the penny belongs to the man who grabs it? Do you think Mishnah is right?

7. Our next Mishnah tells us about what property we find and can keep, and what property we have to try to return to the rightful owner. We all have heard, "Finders keepers, losers weepers." Do you think Mishnah agrees? Does Mishnah agree all of the time, or some of the time, or never? What sorts of things does Mishnah want you to try to return, if you can find the owner? What sorts of things does Mishnah let you keep without trying to find the owner? See if you can predict what Mishnah is going to rule on this very commonplace problem.

Honesty Is The Best Policy But What's Honesty?

MISHNAH BABA MEṢI'A' 2:1-2

Mishnah takes simple problems and shows that they are complicated. The reason is that the oral Torah wants to help us find out what is fair and what is unfair, both fair to other people and fair to ourselves. We do not know automatically or naturally how to be a good person and how to live the way God wants us to. We have to learn how. You already know that.

So let's go back to that penny in the street, to the problem of returning lost property to the rightful owner. Obviously, if you find something on the street and can return it to the one who owns it, you do. Nothing could be simpler than that.

But sometimes you can't find the owner. And sometimes, even if you can find the owner, the owner can't show that he or she really does own the thing you have found. And sometimes no one in the world could rightfully claim to own what you have found, even though anyone would want to try. How do we know the difference? When do we say, "It's not really yours, even though you found it. Finders aren't keepers"? And when do we say, "Yes, you can keep it. Finders are keepers"?

We all know that honesty is the best policy. But what is honesty? What are the requirements of doing the right thing in this most simple and commonplace event of our lives—finding a mitten or a penny or a purse?

This next Mishnah has an idea that is not entirely familiar to us. It says that if you find a certain thing, you have to "proclaim" or announce it. You have to tell people what you have found, so that the rightful owner can step forward and claim the lost property. This is equivalent, in our terms, to trying to find the owner, but it's slightly more specific. It's like putting an ad in the paper announcing that you've found a gold watch. Other things, Mishnah will tell us, you don't have to "proclaim." You can keep what you've found.

Another interesting side to this Mishnah is the way it is put into words. It is in the form of lists: a list of things that you have to proclaim, and then, a list of things that you don't have to proclaim. There are ten items on each list. Then you have to find the principle that is expressed by the ten examples of that single principle.

But the main point of this Mishnah is familiar, even if its choice of words is unfamiliar. It claims that honesty is the best policy, but we have to figure out what being honest demands of us.

MISHNAH BABA MEṢI'A' 2:1-2

אֵלּוּ מְצִיאוֹת שֶׁלּוֹ, וְאֵלּוּ חַיָּב לְהַכְרִיז? אֵלּוּ מְצִיאוֹת שֶׁלּוֹ:
מָצָא פֵרוֹת מְפֻזָּרִין, מָעוֹת מְפֻזָּרוֹת, כְּרִיכוֹת בִּרְשׁוּת הָרַבִּים,
וְעִגּוּלֵי דְבֵלָה, כִּכָּרוֹת שֶׁלְּנַחְתּוֹם, מַחֲרוֹזוֹת שֶׁלְּדָגִים, וַחֲתִיכוֹת
שֶׁלְּבָשָׂר, וְגִזֵּי צֶמֶר הַבָּאוֹת מִמְּדִינָתָן, וַאֲנִיצֵי פִשְׁתָּן, וּלְשׁוֹנוֹת
שֶׁלְּאַרְגָּמָן — הֲרֵי אֵלּוּ שֶׁלּוֹ; דִּבְרֵי רַבִּי מֵאִיר. רַבִּי יְהוּדָה אוֹמֵר:
כָּל שֶׁיֵּשׁ בּוֹ שִׁנּוּי חַיָּב לְהַכְרִיז. כֵּיצַד? מָצָא עָגוּל וּבְתוֹכוֹ חֶרֶס,
כִּכָּר וּבְתוֹכוֹ מָעוֹת. רַבִּי שִׁמְעוֹן בֶּן אֶלְעָזָר אוֹמֵר: כָּל כְּלֵי אַנְפּוֹרְיָא
אֵינוֹ חַיָּב לְהַכְרִיז.   וְאֵלּוּ חַיָּב לְהַכְרִיז: מָצָא פֵרוֹת בַּכְּלִי, אוֹ
כְלִי כְּמוֹת שֶׁהוּא, מָעוֹת בַּכִּיס, אוֹ כִיס כְּמוֹת שֶׁהוּא, צִבּוּרֵי פֵרוֹת,
צִבּוּרֵי מָעוֹת, שְׁלֹשָׁה מַטְבְּעוֹת זֶה עַל גַּב זֶה, כְּרִיכוֹת בִּרְשׁוּת
הַיָּחִיד, וְכִכָּרוֹת שֶׁלְּבַעַל הַבַּיִת, וְגִזֵּי צֶמֶר הַלָּקוּחוֹת מִבֵּית הָאֻמָּן,
כַּדֵּי יַיִן וְכַדֵּי שֶׁמֶן — הֲרֵי אֵלּוּ חַיָּב לְהַכְרִיז.

Vocabulary

what	אֵלּוּ	found	מָצָא
finds	מְצִיאוֹת	fruit	פֵרוֹת
his	שֶׁלּוֹ	scattered	מְפֻזָּרִין
must	חַיָּב	money	מָעוֹת
to proclaim	לְהַכְרִיז	small sheaves	כְּרִיכוֹת

in public property	בִּרְשׁוּת הָרַבִּים	how	כֵּיצַד
cakes (of)	עִגוּלֵי	and in it	וּבְתוֹכוֹ
pressed figs	דְּבֵלָה	potsherd	חֶרֶס
loaves	כִּכָּרוֹת	new merchandise	כְּלֵי אַנְפּוֹרְיָא
baker	נַחְתּוֹם	vessel	כְּלִי
strings	מַחֲרוֹזוֹת	empty	כְּמוֹת שֶׁהוּא
fish	דָּגִים	change purse	כִּיס
pieces	חֲתִיכוֹת	heaps (of)	צִבּוּרֵי
meat	בָּשָׂר	three	שְׁלֹשָׁה
wool-shearings	גִּזֵּי צֶמֶר	coins	מַטְבְּעוֹת
which come	הַבָּאוֹת	in private property	בִּרְשׁוּת הַיָּחִיד
from their country	מִמְּדִינָתָן	home-made	שֶׁלְּבַעַל הַבַּיִת
stalks (of)	אֲנִיצֵי	which is bought	הַלְּקוּחוֹת
flax	פִּשְׁתָּן	from a workshop	מִבֵּית הָאָמָּן
strips	לְשׁוֹנוֹת	jars (of)	כַּדֵּי
purple wool	אַרְגָּמָן	wine	יַיִן
everything	כָּל	oil	שֶׁמֶן
unusual	שָׁנוּי		

How the Mishnah Is Put Together

1 אֵלּוּ מְצִיאוֹת שֶׁלּוֹ,
וְאֵלּוּ חַיָּב לְהַכְרִיז?

What lost property (belongs to) him, and what (lost property) is he liable to proclaim?

2 אֵלּוּ מְצִיאוֹת שֶׁלּוֹ:

מָצָא

These are the (kinds of) lost property (which are) his: (If) he found

53

pieces of fruit (which were) scattered about

פֵּרוֹת מְפֻזָּרִין,

coins scattered about

מָעוֹת מְפֻזָּרוֹת,

loaves of bread in the public way

כְּרִיכוֹת בִּרְשׁוּת הָרַבִּים,

cakes of figs

וְעִגּוּלֵי דְבֵלָה,

loaves of bread of a baker

כִּכָּרוֹת שֶׁלַּנַּחְתּוֹם,

strings of fish

מַחֲרוֹזוֹת שֶׁלְּדָגִים,

pieces of meat

וַחֲתִיכוֹת שֶׁלְּבָשָׂר,

wool-shearings (as) they come from their country

וְגִזֵּי צֶמֶר הַבָּאוֹת מִמְּדִינָתָן,

and stalks of flax

וַאֲנִיצֵי פִשְׁתָּן,

and strips of purple wool

וּלְשׁוֹנוֹת שֶׁלְּאַרְגָּמָן —

lo, these are his,

הֲרֵי אֵלּוּ שֶׁלּוֹ;

the words of Rabbi Meir.

דִּבְרֵי רַבִּי מֵאִיר.

Rabbi Judah says, Whatever has on it a mark (which) changes (its character) he is liable to proclaim.

3 רַבִּי יְהוּדָה אוֹמֵר: כָּל שֶׁיֵּשׁ בּוֹ שִׁנּוּי חַיָּב לְהַכְרִיז.

How so? (If) he found a fig-cake and in it is a sherd

4 כֵּיצַד? מָצָא עִגּוּל וּבְתוֹכוֹ חֶרֶס,

a loaf and in it are coins (he must proclaim it).

כִּכָּר וּבְתוֹכוֹ מָעוֹת.

Rabbi Simeon ben Eleazar says, All (new) merchandise he does not have to proclaim.

5 רַבִּי שִׁמְעוֹן בֶּן אֶלְעָזָר אוֹמֵר: כָּל כְּלֵי אַנְפּוּרְיָא אֵינוֹ חַיָּב לְהַכְרִיז.

headline announces the topic of both Mishnahs. It asks a question: What are the sorts of lost property which belong to the finders, and what are the sorts of lost property which the finder is supposed to "proclaim"? When does someone have to put up a notice or take an ad in the lost and found? The rest of the first Mishnah answers the first part of the question.

Let's notice how the entire Mishnah is put together and be sure we know the meaning of each of its parts. First we see that the Mishnah is a list of ten things, and the corresponding Mishnah, which we'll see in a moment, also lists ten things. But then our Mishnah has two other opinions, Nos. 3 and 4. Judah's opinion, No. 3, is explained at No. 4, and finally we have No. 5, which really is separate from everything which already has been said. It is a bit of information thrown in but serves no real purpose.

You notice that the question is answered by Meir. He gives a list of ten items. Judah also answers a question. But he gives no list at all. Judah wants to tell us about the sorts of lost property which one *must* proclaim. Does he disagree with Meir? Hardly. He isn't even talking about the same thing. It would be better if Judah's saying in Nos. 3 and 4 were moved to the bottom of the Mishnah we shall see in a moment. And so, too, should Simeon ben Eleazar's saying be moved down, since he too is not talking about the same thing as Meir in No. 2.

And this brings us to Meir's list. What are his ten items? He starts, "(If) someone found"—and then gives us ten things a person might find, followed by, "Lo, these belong to the finder." These ten things are: scattered fruit; scattered money, that is, pennies thrown this way and that; small bundles of food in the road (which, we know, belongs to everybody); cakes of figs; loaves of bread made by a baker; strings of fish; pieces of meat; wool-shearings brought from the country (that is, not yet worked over); stalks of flax; strips of purple wool.

Obviously, Meir is telling us about things which people found in his day. To discover what he would say about things we might find in our day, we have to ask, "What do Meir's things have in common?" The answer is obvious. These are things which have no mark or sign that they belong to some particular person. Even if you went around and said, "I found a quarter," could anybody prove ownership of the quarter? Hardly. What, after all, could someone say about a quarter? A quarter is a quarter. It has no distinguishing mark, nothing about which you could say, "Look—I lost it, and the sign that it is mine is that it has my name on it," or, "It has a mark on it which I made with a pen." None of these things bears any special sign or mark. If you find any of them, you can keep it without any further trouble.

Judah, in No. 3, then says something which Meir certainly should accept. He says, "Anything on which is some unusual mark—you have to proclaim it." What does Judah mean? We look back to No. 4 to find the answer. Someone found a fig-cake, but inside it is a sherd—a piece of a jar. Now, if you lost the fig-cake, you could say, "I lost a fig-cake, and I marked it with a sherd of a clay jar." Anyone would know, "Yes, that must be his. It is that mark which he himself put there." Or if you found a loaf of bread with a coin inside, you could claim, "But that's mine. I recognize it, because I put a penny inside it." These things do belong to someone, and we know it because, as Judah says, there is some identifying mark.

You lose your book. You know it's your book, because inside the front cover you wrote—not your name, because then, obviously, it's yours, but your initials. Or you drew a picture of your house, or made some mark which indicates that the book belongs to you. Judah and Meir agree on the principle.

If you had to pick out the two items on Meir's list that interest Judah, which ones would you choose? Obviously, they would be fig-cakes and bread loaves, the two things to which Judah refers explicitly. So Meir and Judah can be working with the same couple of obvious examples of the point on which both agree.

This brings us down to Simeon ben Eleazar. He has one lonely item. He refers to something that is new, just purchased in the store. If you find on the street a toy which still has its price tag, do you have to announce it? No, Simeon says, you don't. Why not? Because the owner has not yet made a mark on the toy. It can belong to anybody. Anyone who walked into the store could have bought the toy. But Simeon's opinion probably would not please Meir and Judah, because, so far as they are concerned, there may be some sort of special mark on the toy which allows the loser to say, "That's the one I lost." So Simeon wants more than some distinguishing mark. He wants solid evidence.

Let's go on to the second Mishnah, the list of ten things that you do have to proclaim to try to find the rightful owner of the lost property. The list of ten things is exactly in the model of the first list: "These are things which one has to proclaim: (If) someone found" and then come the ten things, followed by, "Behold, these are the things which one is supposed to proclaim." Here is the Mishnah once more.

MISHNAH BABA MEṢI'A'　2

And these is he liable to proclaim: (If) he found	וְאֵלּוּ חַיָּב לְהַכְרִיז: מָצָא
1. pieces of fruit in a utensil or an empty utensil	1　פֵּרוֹת בִּכְלִי, אוֹ כְלִי כְּמוֹת שֶׁהוּא,
2. coins in a change-purse or an empty change-purse	2　מָעוֹת בַּכִּיס, אוֹ כִיס כְּמוֹת שֶׁהוּא,
3. heaps of fruit	3　צִבּוּרֵי פֵרוֹת,
4. heaps of coins	4　צִבּוּרֵי מָעוֹת,
5. three coins on top of one another	5　שְׁלֹשָׁה מַטְבְּעוֹת זֶה עַל גַּב זֶה,
6. loaves of bread on private property	6　כְּרִיכוֹת בִּרְשׁוּת הַיָּחִיד,
7. loaves of bread baked at home	7　וְכִכָּרוֹת שֶׁלְּבַעַל הַבַּיִת,
8. wool-shearings bought from a wool-worker's shop	8　וְגִזֵּי צֶמֶר הַלְּקוּחוֹת מִבֵּית הָאֻמָּן,
9. jars of wine	9　כַּדֵּי יַיִן
10. jars of olive-oil	10　וְכַדֵּי שֶׁמֶן —
lo, these must he proclaim	הֲרֵי אֵלּוּ חַיָּב לְהַכְרִיז.

hat are these ten things? Item 1 speaks of pieces of fruit that you find in a utensil. For instance, you find apples in a basket. You have to try to find the owner. Why? Because no one is going to put apples into a basket and then leave them somewhere. The person who puts the apples into the basket wants those apples. Then we have a second example. If you find an empty basket, that too belongs to someone. Item 2 refers to money in a money-purse. Obviously, someone is looking for that purse. If you find an empty purse, you should look for the owner. There was money in it, which, presumably, has been removed. But the purse, too, is valuable, and the owner wants it back. Items 3, 4 and 5 are simple. You find a pile of fruit or a pile of money. Does someone want them? Of course. These things have been carefully arranged. Someone can easily say, "I know they're mine, because I piled them up just that way." And he or she can say so even before you say where the things are, or before he or she can see how they're piled up. Item 6 matches item 3 in the earlier Mishnah. There we referred to sheaves in the public way. Here we have sheaves on private property, in your yard. Obviously, these belong to someone who will want to come back and get them if possible.

Item 7 speaks of homemade loaves of bread. Whoever bakes bread at home makes it in a particular way. There's no single mold for all bread. So it is easy to identify. Item 8 contrasts with item 8 on the former list. We have wool-shearings bought from the shop of someone who works the wool. Items 9 and 10 are obvious. You find a jug of wine or oil. Certainly these things belong to someone.

So far, we have taken one line of thought. We have emphasized that the things you have to try to return have some distinguishing mark, just as Judah says. Things you *don't* have to return are commonplace and can belong to anybody. They have nothing special about them.

WHAT IS OWNERLESS PROPERTY?

There is a second thing to consider. That is: What is the *attitude* of the original owner toward this lost property? Does the owner hope to get it back or not? How can we know? And why is this important?

Let's start with the question of whether the owner hopes to get the property back. People are realistic. They know that if they drop some money on the street, there is little chance they'll ever see it again. Why? Because even if someone went looking, how could the original owner know that this was *the* lost money? He or she wouldn't have any idea. Anyone can pick up pennies in the street. So when you find loose pennies on the street, you have every reason to think that the owner is not now thinking, "Oh, when am I going to get my money back"? The owner is realistic and knows that he or she will never see it again. No one hopes to find that money. It's gone. Those pennies belong to no one.

If, on the other hand, the owner leaves the money tied up in a handkerchief, then that's a different story. If someone does go around saying, "I've found some money in a handkerchief" or "in a change-purse," and you can show that the handkerchief or change-purse really does belong to you—it has your initials sewn into it—then you're going to get that money back. So you don't give up hope.

How do we know whether or not our unknown owner has given up hope? We know *the same way* that we know whether or not we have to look for the owner. If there is some distinguishing mark, then the owner may well expect to find them again. But if the apples are just scattered around on the ground, the owner can't possibly expect to find them. And even if you found the owner, there is no way that he could prove the apples belong to him.

This brings us to the last and most important question: Why is the owner's attitude—or, we have to say, why is our *guess* about the owner's attitude—so important in telling us what we have to do with lost property?

The answer is simple.

Is this really ownerless property, which we can just pick up and take for ourselves? If it is, then it's there for the taking. We're not stealing. In all honesty, we can pick up those apples and know that they don't belong to anybody else, so they might as well belong to us.

That's the case if we find something that someone else can't possibly think is his. But what if the owner still is looking for the property and still thinks that it belongs to him? Then if we take it and make it our own, we are doing nothing other than stealing.

And that's the important consideration here. *We have to look around for the owner when there is reason to believe that the owner still regards the object as his or her own.* And we don't have to look around for the owner when there is no reason in the world to believe that the owner still regards the object as his own. So everything depends upon your attitude, a point which is hardly going to surprise you at this stage in your learning of Mishnah.

WHAT DOES IT MEAN TO ME?

The first thing you learn is what to do when you find something on the street. You have responsibilities to other people. But these responsibilities are not without limit. There are things you have to do, and things you don't have to do. If you find a tennis ball and it's like all other tennis balls—it's yours. Keep it. No one can possibly claim it, because even if someone did, how would the person prove it really belonged to him?

If you find a tennis ball that is painted purple, or that has an initial on it, you have to go and tell people, "Did anyone lose a tennis ball?" And if someone says, "I lost a tennis ball, and it has the initial X on it," you know whose ball it is.

Why does something belong to the finder? Because it doesn't belong to anyone else. Why does something *not* belong to the finder? Because it still belongs to someone else.

The reason there are things you can keep is that there are things that, once lost, are not going to be found again by the owner. So the owner gives up hope of finding them. His or her attitude toward the lost property affects it. Once the owner gives up hope of finding what has been lost, then the lost property is there for anyone to take and keep. And, it follows, you can take it and make it your own.

But if you have reason to believe the owner still hopes to find what is lost, then that tennis ball that you found is not ownerless property. It still belongs to someone, somewhere, and that means you have to try to find the owner. It's as simple as that.

And there's one last point. Since everything depends upon the attitude of the owner, you have to figure out how to guess what that attitude is. Why? Because you don't know the owner, and you can't ask what he or she is thinking! That's the basis for the problem. So in the end, the person's attitude is *your* attitude. And that is where you need the kind of guidance that Mishnah gives you. What you think someone else is thinking is what makes all the difference in the world.

1. Why is it fair to ask someone who claims to be the owner of a tennis ball to prove that he or she really is the owner? Why don't you just give the tennis ball you found to anyone who claims it?
2. What does Mishnah mean when it speaks about having to "proclaim" that you found an object? What language would you use for the same thing? What are the things you would do in order to "proclaim" that you found something? Are these things which people ordinarily do if they're honest?
3. Why does Mishnah like to make lists? Are these lists easy to memorize? Can you make up a list of ten things which you have to proclaim and ten things which you don't have to proclaim?
5. Do you think that Simeon will agree with Judah and Meir? Do you think that he has a good point? Is his viewpoint relevant to the world you know?
6. What is the point in common among all of the things which are on Meir's list? What is the point in common among all of the things which are on the list of the second Mishnah?
7. Why does Mishnah think that you have a right to keep some lost property that you find, but you have to try to find the owner of other sorts of lost property that you find? What is the basic principle behind all of these rules?
8. Mishnah's idea is that you have to protect yourself, not

only the other person. What does Mishnah want to protect you from doing? Which of the Ten Commandments stands behind our Mishnah?

9. If Mishnah seems to want to spell out the requirements of one of the Ten Commandments, then what is the relationship of Mishnah, the oral Torah, to the Ten Commandments of the written Torah? Can you say that the oral Torah wants to spell out the meaning of the written Torah?

10. Mishnah's real interest is in showing not only fairness, but something more important than fairness. What really interests Mishnah? Why is it so important to Mishnah that you be saved from doing the wrong thing?

PART THREE

The Holy and the Extraordinary

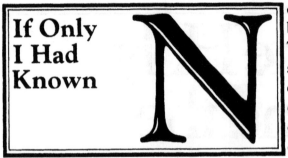

If Only I Had Known

Now we turn to less practical but still important matters. They concern our relationships with God and with other people, rather than everyday and ordinary events. They fall into the category of the holy because

MISHNAH NEDARIM 9:1-2 they concern extraordinary matters, like how you keep your word, what you do when you swear or vow, and how you do those things which are matters of religion. The Torah is interested in what we do and say to other people and what we say to God. Because words are just as important as deeds. You can hurt someone just as much by saying something mean as you can by handing out a knock in the ribs or by kicking. In fact, you can hurt more. You can sin as much by lying as by stealing, as much by swearing you'll do something and then not doing it as by keeping for yourself what belongs to someone else. All of these things are matters of holiness. Because God cares for us and loves us, God is interested in the things we do and in the things we say.

Our first problem has to do with swearing. Sometimes you say, whether you're glad or angry, "I swear I'll never do it again." Or: "I vow I'll never speak to you again." Then, later on, you are sorry. You say, "If I had known, I should never have said it." So what? Does that let you out of your oath? You've tied yourself up in a knot. How do you untie that knot? This is the issue before us. But let's start back at the basic principle.

Mishnah says that the most important thing about you is your attitude. Everything depends on how you intend things to be. But *what* is your attitude? How do you express it? The answer is obvious. It comes out in what you say. (We know the other half of the answer: It comes out in what you do.)

Everything begins in words: love and war, friendship and fights. First of all, we love and have fights in the family. That is why Mishnah's third division, on the family, is about words. And the third division wants to tell us that the family is built on words—words a man and a woman say to each other that make them a married couple, words that break up their marriage.

The family is a world of promises we make and keep, or make and break.

That brings us to the problem of saying something in anger or in enthusiasm, something that, later on, we're sorry we ever said.

Sometimes we get angry at our brother or sister and say something mean. There are limits to what we'll say to an outsider. But there are no limits to what we'll say to our family. But sometimes we say something we regret, and we're sorry about it. How do we deal with this? What do we do when we're sorry?

And, above all, what are the right grounds for being sorry? Can we just say anything we want and know that later on we can get out of it? We know we can't. We know there are limits because—as we'll see—Yom Kippur—that powerful day, isn't strong enough to overcome some words we might say.

So we have to ask, "What are the grounds for getting out of something we've said? How do we turn the world around by words?" To understand Mishnah's answer we must know that in the time of Mishnah there was a way people commonly exploded in words. They would take a vow. They would say, "Such and so is forbidden to me!" "Such and so is to me as if it were holy and reserved to God!" "Such and so is off limits to me!" "Such and such is *Qonam*" prohibited.

And that vow meant that what they had mentioned, or the person they had mentioned, would be off limits. You could not make use of the thing. You could not accept a favor from the person.

Our ancestors were emotional people. And so are we. We don't hide our feelings. We express them. So it is not uncommon for them, and for us, to explode in such words. But the result is not always happy. Because later on people regret what they said. They wish they hadn't said it. Yet being people who believe the word is sacred and holy, we can't just say, "Oh well—forget it!" We can't forget it.

So in olden times they would go to a wise man, a rabbi, and ask him to undo the words they had said. Now what could he do? Well, the wise rabbis of the day—the sages—would try to figure out grounds for untying the knot of words that people had tied around themselves. The Mishnah before us shows how the sages tried to solve this problem.

MISHNAH NEDARIM 9:1-2

רַבִּי אֱלִיעֶזֶר אוֹמֵר: פּוֹתְחִין לְאָדָם בִּכְבוֹד אָבִיו וְאִמּוֹ;
וַחֲכָמִים אוֹסְרִין. אָמַר רַבִּי צָדוֹק: עַד שֶׁפּוֹתְחִין לוֹ בִּכְבוֹד אָבִיו
וְאִמּוֹ, יִפְתְּחוּ לוֹ בִּכְבוֹד הַמָּקוֹם, אִם כֵּן אֵין נְדָרִים! וּמוֹדִים
חֲכָמִים לְרַבִּי אֱלִיעֶזֶר בְּדָבָר שֶׁבֵּינוֹ לְבֵין אָבִיו וְאִמּוֹ, שֶׁפּוֹתְחִין לוֹ
בִּכְבוֹד אָבִיו וְאִמּוֹ.   וְעוֹד אָמַר רַבִּי אֱלִיעֶזֶר: פּוֹתְחִין בַּנּוֹלָד;
וַחֲכָמִים אוֹסְרִין. כֵּיצַד? אָמַר: קוֹנָם שֶׁאֵינִי נֶהֱנֶה לְאִישׁ פְּלוֹנִי,
וְנַעֲשָׂה סוֹפֵר, אוֹ שֶׁהָיָה מַשִּׂיא אֶת בְּנוֹ בְּקָרוֹב, וְאָמַר: אִלּוּ הָיִיתִי
יוֹדֵעַ שֶׁהוּא נַעֲשֶׂה סוֹפֵר, אוֹ שֶׁהוּא מַשִּׂיא אֶת בְּנוֹ בְּקָרוֹב — לֹא
הָיִיתִי נוֹדֵר. קוֹנָם לַבַּיִת זֶה שֶׁאֵינִי נִכְנָס, וְנַעֲשָׂה בֵּית הַכְּנֶסֶת,
אָמַר: אִלּוּ הָיִיתִי יוֹדֵעַ שֶׁהוּא נַעֲשֶׂה בֵּית הַכְּנֶסֶת, לֹא הָיִיתִי
נוֹדֵר — רַבִּי אֱלִיעֶזֶר מַתִּיר; וַחֲכָמִים אוֹסְרִין.

Vocabulary

open	פּוֹתְחִין	agree	מוֹדִים
man	אָדָם	between	בֵּין
for the honor	בִּכְבוֹד	the future	נוֹלָד
his father	אָבִיו	how	כֵּיצַד
his mother	אִמּוֹ	benefit	נֶהֱנֶה
sages	חֲכָמִים	person	אִישׁ
forbid	אוֹסְרִין	such-and-such	פְּלוֹנִי
until	עַד	became	נַעֲשָׂה
the Lord	הַמָּקוֹם	scribe	סוֹפֵר
if	אִם	marry	מַשִּׂיא
so	כֵּן	soon	בְּקָרוֹב
vows	נְדָרִים	if	אִלּוּ

know	יוֹדֵעַ	synagogue	בֵּית הַכְּנֶסֶת
vow	נוֹדֵר	permits	מַתִּיר
enter	נִכְנָס		

How the Mishnah Is Put Together

1 Rabbi Eliezer says:

רַבִּי אֱלִיעֶזֶר אוֹמֵר:

They untie (a vow) for a person on account of the honor of his father and his mother.

פּוֹתְחִין לָאָדָם בִּכְבוֹד אָבִיו וְאִמּוֹ;

And sages prohibit (keep it tied).

וַחֲכָמִים אוֹסְרִין.

2 Said Rabbi Sadoq:

אָמַר רַבִּי צָדוֹק:

Before they untie (a vow) for him on account of his father and his mother,

עַד שֶׁפּוֹתְחִין לוֹ בִּכְבוֹד אָבִיו וְאִמּוֹ,

let them untie it for him on account of the honor of the Omnipresent.

יִפְתְּחוּ לוֹ בִּכְבוֹד הַמָּקוֹם,

(And) if so, there will be no vows (at all)!

אִם כֵּן אֵין נְדָרִים!

3 Sages agree with Rabbi Eliezer concerning a matter (about which he vowed) between his father and his mother, that they untie it for him on account of the honor of his father and his mother.

וּמוֹדִים חֲכָמִים לְרַבִּי אֱלִיעֶזֶר בְּדָבָר שֶׁבֵּינוֹ לְבֵין אָבִיו וְאִמּוֹ, שֶׁפּוֹתְחִין לוֹ בִּכְבוֹד אָבִיו וְאִמּוֹ.

ur Mishnah is in three distinct parts. It is complete in No. 1. We have Eliezer's rule, and the sages' disagreement with it. Then Sadoq makes his comment on Eliezer's opinion. Then the little discussion between Eliezer and sages resumes in No. 3. Sadoq has interrupted the discussion. (This is an "interpolation"—something which is inserted into a complete and whole unit of thought.) Sages agree on one part of Eliezer's opinion.

Let's ask what Eliezer wants to tell us. His point is this: What are proper grounds for saying, "It isn't binding"? You're not tied up in knots by words when you can find a way of untying the knots. And one way, Eliezer says (he's going to give us some more ways in a moment) is this:

You say, "If I had known what would come about, I'd never have said such a thing."

That, in general, is not enough (in a moment, Eliezer is going to tell us that it *is* enough) to untie the knot.

But if you say, "You know, what I said has brought shame on my father and my mother," that is enough to untie the knot.

So from Eliezer's viewpoint, there are things which are more important than the vow, the very word which makes a family into a family. What is more important than the word is the family itself: the mother and the father.

Sadoq rightly objects to Eliezer's view. He says, "Why stop with the family—with the mother and the father?" After all, God makes us all. If we say something which brings dishonor to God, then that should be sufficient grounds to untie the knot of words.

"But," Sadoq continues, "If you say *that,* then there never can be a vow again." Why not? Because any sort of vow which leads to inconvenience or embarrassment will be untied. All you have to say is, "God's honor is involved." "So," Sadoq says, "Eliezar's opinion leads to making a joke of words."

In No. 3, sages come back and change their minds, but only a little.

They say, "Well, we can't take Eliezer's view of grounds for dissolving a vow. Sadoq has a point. But if a person makes a vow that has to do with the father or the mother in particular, and if the person then finds that the honor owing to the father and the mother is hurt, then you can untie the vow." For, after all, the Torah commands us to honor father and mother. So a vow which hurts them—a vow, for example, that you won't give your mother a kiss "ever again" because you're angry at her!—has no standing to begin with. You can't, after all, take a vow to God not to do one of the rules of God's Torah. So that vow, sages agree with Eliezer, is not valid. It is untied because it never was a knot to begin with. Sages don't concede much.

MISHNAH NEDARIM 9:2

1	And furthermore did Rabbi Eliezer say:	וְעוֹד אָמַר רַבִּי אֱלִיעֶזֶר:
	They untie (a vow) on account of something which happened (later on)	פּוֹתְחִין בַּנּוֹלָד;
	And sages prohibit	וַחֲכָמִים אוֹסְרִין.
	How so?	כֵּיצַד?
2	(If) he said, *Qonam*—that I shall not derive benefit from so-and-so	אָמַר: קוֹנָם שֶׁאֵינִי נֶהֱנֶה לְאִישׁ פְּלוֹנִי,
	and he (so-and-so) became a scribe	וְנַעֲשָׂה סוֹפֵר,
3	or was going to marry off his son very soon	אוֹ שֶׁהָיָה מַשִּׂיא אֶת בְּנוֹ בְקָרוֹב,
	and he said, If I had known that he would become a scribe	וְאָמַר: אִלּוּ הָיִיתִי יוֹדֵעַ שֶׁהוּא נַעֲשָׂה סוֹפֵר,
	or that he would marry off his son very soon	אוֹ שֶׁהוּא מַשִּׂיא אֶת בְּנוֹ בְקָרוֹב —

I should not have taken a vow	לֹא הָיִיתִי נוֹדֵר.
Qonam against this house, that I shall not enter it	4 קוֹנָם לְבַיִת זֶה שֶׁאֵינִי נִכְנָס,
and it was made into a synagogue	וְנַעֲשָׂה בֵית הַכְּנֶסֶת,
(if) he said, If I had known that it would be made into a synagogue, I should not have taken a vow	אָמַר: אִלּוּ הָיִיתִי יוֹדֵעַ שֶׁהוּא נַעֲשֶׂה בֵית הַכְּנֶסֶת, לֹא הָיִיתִי נוֹדֵר —
Rabbi Eliezer unties (the vow)	5 רַבִּי אֱלִיעֶזֶר מַתִּיר;
And sages prohibit (keep it tied).	וַחֲכָמִים אוֹסְרִין.

e go over the same ground again. But now Eliezer has a much more sweeping opinion. And surely, Sadoq would exclaim, "If so, there never will be vows again!"

For Eliezer now says, "You can untie a vow when you see what happens later on." Sages say this is no ground for untying the knot. We don't have to explain what Eliezer means, because our Mishnah immediately tells us.

It says, 'How so'? Then it proceeds to give three examples.

No. 2 is the first example. The man says, "I'll have nothing to do with Bill." But then Bill becomes a scribe, and Joe needs to make use of the scribe's services. It's easy enough to translate this into our own times. "Bill, I'll never speak to you again!" Then Bill becomes pitcher of your baseball team, and you're catcher. You have to speak to him.

No. 3 gives us a new example, but it refers to the example in No. 2. The man was marrying off his son (or daughter, of course). Now you've said, "I'll never talk to you again!" But you want to go to the wedding. In fact—remember, we're talking about families—you *have* to go to the wedding, or everyone will wonder why you're not there.

No. 4 follows the same lines. There's a house in which you have a bad experience. Perhaps someone lives there, and you go to visit, and your friend is mean to you that day. You say, "I'll never walk into this house again!" But your (former) friend moves away. A few years later, a group of Jews buys the building and turns it into a synagogue. Naturally, you want to go there, because you're one of the group. And you remember what you said in such a different situation, so many years ago.

In all three cases, you say, "If only I had known. . . ." "If only I had known before I spoke that Bill would become a scribe," "if only I had known before I spoke that Uncle Joe would marry off my cousin Johnny," "if only I had known before I spoke that that building a year from now would not stand for all the bad things it means to me now"—if only I had known, then what?

Eliezer unties the knot.

Sages keep it tied.

There is an interesting disagreement here. When there is a difference of opinion in Mishnah, it's because each side has something worthwhile to say. There is right on both sides.

Eliezer's believes that if a vow is to stay tied it has to mean something. You must know, for all time, exactly what you're saying. Because you give your word, and in order to keep it, you must want to keep it forever. If you discover later on that there were things you didn't know when you said what you said, that means that at the outset you could *not* have meant what you said.

Since you didn't mean it—so you find out later on—then you didn't say a thing. And it's null and void. That's a fair position, because, after all, you can't be bound to your mistakes, and you can rightly claim to be able to correct your mistakes.

Sages take a different view, and they're right too. They say—just as Sadoq says—if you can always weasel out of things you say, then what's the point of taking a vow at all! "What you're saying, Eliezer, is that a person always can get out of what he or she says, that you can always untie the knot. But then, Eliezer, all you're saying is that a knot is never tied." That means people really are not *responsible* for what they say. It means a person's word spoken in anger is nothing.

But people do speak in anger. They do say things in enthusiasm. They do express their warm feelings. Is all this nothing? "What you're saying, Eliezer, is more than what you think you're saying. You think you're saying that if you find out you didn't mean it, then it's as if you didn't say it. But what you're really saying is that you never *have* to mean it. You can always untie the knot of words."

Underneath this disagreement, there's another disagreement. Eliezer has a low view of people. He doesn't really respect them because, so far as he is concerned, you don't really have to take them seriously. You can discount, for some reason, whatever people say. People are excitable. They're always popping off. So just let it pass, and don't pay attention. They'll be sorry. You don't hold them to their word. You don't keep them tied up to anything they say because, anyhow, they're excitable and undependable. You just take that into account and turn your back.

Deep down, sages have a high view of people. They really do respect them. You take seriously what people say. True, that leads to some tough decisions. But if you respect people, you take them at face value. You do say, "Well, you said it. You have a right to say it. I listen to you, and I take you seriously. So—now you can choke on it! *But I won't treat you like a baby.* I listen to you, and I respect you. Therefore your words are something I value."

WHAT DOES IT MEAN TO ME?

Let's start with the disagreement between Eliezer and sages. Both sides are right, and they're right about us.

Eliezer is right. We do say things which later on we regret. We're sorry because we see the result of what we said. We say, "If only I had known, I should never have said it."

Words spoken in anger—how we wish we could reach out, catch them and put them back into our pockets! How many times we say to our brothers or sisters, our mothers or fathers, our friends, "I swear I'll never talk to you again!" Or we just say, "I won't play with you again." And then, five minutes later, we're smiling and happy.

But we *did* say those words.

Eliezer tells us, "Okay, you said them. But if you had known then what you know now, would you have said them? Obviously, not. So forget it. It's as if you said nothing."

Sages are right too. We want people to listen to us. We don't want them to dismiss us. "Oh, well—Kevin's only a child." "Melissa's only a little girl, so she doesn't know what she's saying."

In fact, we not only want people to take us seriously, we want to take ourselves seriously.

That means *we want and need to think, when we speak, that we mean what we say.* Come what may, we'll stick by what we say because, whatever other people think or don't think about us, we believe we're worth listening to. If we don't, we shouldn't talk.

Our warm feelings—sometimes of love, sometimes of anger—get in our way. But they have to because the price of caring is sometimes making promises we can't keep, sometimes saying things we can't carry out.

Other people do it too, and they do it to us. They, too, make promises—make a "vow," in Mishnah's language—for which they're sorry. Do we let them untie the knot? Do we untie the knot for them?

This is a painful problem because there's no simple and obvious answer. You just have to weigh things in the balance. Eliezer's right, and sages are right—and we have to live with both of them. Because, as I said, we can't live if we're always going to be tied up in knots of words. We can't live with people if every word we ever say is going to follow us and keep after us. But we also can't live with ourselves, or with anyone else, if nothing we say ever matters. If words we use or words we hear are just ideas which float in the air, if they don't bind me to you and you to me, then what is reliable? What can you depend on, in the other person, or in yourself?

There are some knots which you can't untie. And one of them is the knot of words.

1. Do you remember about memorizing? Can you memorize the two Mishnahs we have been working on? What are the

things which help you memorize them? Does it help to know that the first Mishnah is in three parts? Isn't Sadoq's objection logical? What are the key words which occur in all three parts? What are the three examples in the second Mishnah?

2. How are your ties to other people expressed in words? What are the promises you make to your friends? Do you put them into words?

3. What are the warm feelings which you put into words? How do they take the form of "vows"—promises? Do you swear?

4. Why does God care about your promises? Why is it important to Mishnah to pay attention to the words you say to others? Do you use God's name when you make a promise?

5. If you don't explode into words, what happens to you? Can you keep your feelings inside all the time, or do they come out sometimes? Is it better to let them come out when you feel those feelings, or is it better to keep them bottled up?

6. Why is it reasonable to say, "If only I had known, I wouldn't have said it"? Does it matter that if you had known in advance what actually would happen, you wouldn't have made a promise which now you can't keep?

7. What does this have to do with your attitude? Why does Mishnah think that the promises you make are shaped by your deepest attitudes? Why does Eliezer take account of your feelings after you have expressed them?

8. You don't want to be treated "like a baby." What do people say or do to treat you like a baby? How is this tied up to untying knots of words?

9. You want to be treated with respect. Everyone does. What does it mean to you to be treated with respect? How do people show that they respect you?

10. If people listen to you and take seriously the things you think and say, what do you owe them? What are your responsibilities to people who take you seriously? How do you take yourself seriously?

74

So What's New?

MISHNAH ROSH HASHSHANAH 1:1

We have concentrated on Mishnahs which talk directly to us about the world in which we live. But Mishnah was put into writing nearly two thousand years ago. And Mishnah tells us things that people were thinking about long before Mishnah itself was written down. After all, Mishnah is Torah, and Torah begins at Sinai.

You would get a false view of Mishnah if you thought that Mishnah *always* talks about our own lives in our own terms. Now it's time to learn a Mishnah that talks about problems we know, but in language which is not familiar to us. It has something important to tell us, something that we have to understand and take seriously. Learning Mishnah is not always easy, and now it is time to learn about the familiar in unfamiliar terms.

Every day is someone's birthday. There's something new every day. It's important to celebrate something each new day so we don't take the world for granted. If we do take the world for granted, we lose our gift to celebrate, to be surprised and happy and amazed at something special. When we forget how to celebrate, we forget how to enjoy life. We get bored, and we grow tired. Seeing what is new, day by day, keeps us alive and vital.

There's another side of things. Every day there is a fresh start in some way of life. We don't always walk on the same old path. We don't have to repeat what we did: our mistakes, our failures, our errors. We have a chance, every day, to start again.

We all know Rosh Hashshanah. We call it New Year or "the Jewish New Year." But Rosh Hashshanah is only one *rosh hashshanah,* only one of many new years, new beginnings. It is the new year for people, the day on which we get a fresh start.

There are other new years. Many things run through cycles. Your birthday is your new year. Your parents' wedding anniversary is the new year of your family. If your family bought a car, then that day, a year later, is a new year for your car. You start a new year of school once every year. You know that that new year starts off one cycle, which is different from—let us say—the new year that begins when your dog has a birthday. (In our house we celebrate our dog's birthday, because he's one of us.) You also start a new year when you plant seeds for flowers in the spring. And you start a new year every four years for the American president on inauguration day. You start a new year for the United States on the Fourth of July, or for Canada on Dominion Day.

Mishnah wants to talk about new years. This is how it tells us about the ones it knows.

MISHNAH
ROSH HASHSHANAH 1:1

אַרְבָּעָה רָאשֵׁי שָׁנִים הֵם: בְּאֶחָד בְּנִיסָן רֹאשׁ הַשָּׁנָה לַמְּלָכִים וְלָרְגָלִים; בְּאֶחָד בֶּאֱלוּל רֹאשׁ הַשָּׁנָה לְמַעְשַׂר בְּהֵמָה. רַבִּי אֶלְעָזָר וְרַבִּי שִׁמְעוֹן אוֹמְרִים: בְּאֶחָד בְּתִשְׁרֵי; בְּאֶחָד בְּתִשְׁרֵי רֹאשׁ הַשָּׁנָה לְשָׁנִים וְלַשְּׁמִטִּין וְלַיּוֹבְלוֹת, לַנְּטִיעָה וְלַיְרָקוֹת, בְּאֶחָד בִּשְׁבָט רֹאשׁ הַשָּׁנָה לָאִילָן, כְּדִבְרֵי בֵית שַׁמַּאי. בֵּית הִלֵּל אוֹמְרִים: בַּחֲמִשָּׁה עָשָׂר בּוֹ.

Vocabulary

four	אַרְבָּעָה	for release years	לַשְּׁמִטִּין
new years	רָאשֵׁי שָׁנִים	for jubilee years	לַיּוֹבְלוֹת
on the first	בְּאֶחָד	for planting	לַנְּטִיעָה
for kings	לַמְּלָכִים	for vegetables	לַיְרָקוֹת
for festivals	לָרְגָלִים	for tree	לָאִילָן
for tithe	לְמַעְשַׂר	words (of)	דִבְרֵי
cattle	בְּהֵמָה	on the fifteenth	בַּחֲמִשָּׁה עָשָׂר
for years	לְשָׁנִים		

How the Mishnah Is Put Together

There are four new years:	אַרְבָּעָה. רָאשֵׁי שָׁנִים הֵם:	
On the first of Nisan	בְּאֶחָד בְּנִיסָן	1
is the new year for kings (governments)	רֹאשׁ הַשָּׁנָה לַמְּלָכִים	
and for festivals	וְלָרְגָלִים;	
On the first of Elul	בְּאֶחָד בֶּאֱלוּל	2
is the new year for the tithe of cattle.	רֹאשׁ הַשָּׁנָה לְמַעְשַׂר בְּהֵמָה.	
Rabbi Eleazar and Rabbi Simeon say,	רַבִּי אֶלְעָזָר וְרַבִּי שִׁמְעוֹן אוֹמְרִים:	
It is on the first of Tishré.	בְּאֶחָד בְּתִשְׁרֵי;	
On the first of Tishré is the new year for years, for years of release, and for jubilees	בְּאֶחָד בְּתִשְׁרֵי רֹאשׁ הַשָּׁנָה לַשָּׁנִים וְלַשְּׁמִטִּין וְלַיּוֹבְלוֹת,	3
and for planting trees and vegetables	לַנְּטִיעָה וְלַיְרָקוֹת;	
On the first of Shevat	בְּאֶחָד בִּשְׁבָט	4
is the new year for a tree, in accord with the words of the House of Shammai.	רֹאשׁ הַשָּׁנָה לָאִילָן, כְּדִבְרֵי בֵית שַׁמַּאי.	
The House of Hillel say, It is on the fifteen of that month.	בֵּית הִלֵּל אוֹמְרִים: בַּחֲמִשָּׁה עָשָׂר בּוֹ.	

77

nce more, let's dissect our little Mishnah-poem. First, we notice that Mishnah tells us how to do it. We don't have to look for ourselves. It announces that it is going to tell us four things, four new years. While the poem is divided into its four units, we also notice that—as usual—we are given threes, that is, nine, a multiple of three. The three threes are not laid out in equal parts. But we can easily remember the nine new years. There are some disagreements, but they don't spoil the poem as a whole. They also don't upset its balance and order.

We certainly have a busy year—nine birthdays, nine new years. To learn exactly what they are, we have to remember that the Jewish calendar runs along its own course, which is different from the secular calendar. Its months have their own names. We need to learn only four, and the secular months to which they correspond:

Nisan	(Roughly) April
Elul	(Roughly) August
Tishré	(Roughly) September
Shebat	(Roughly) January

There is a new year at the beginning of each of these four months. The years are new for different reasons.

I. *Nisan*

On the first day of Nisan what do we celebrate? What begins?

The first thing that begins is the "new year of kings," that is, of governments. Our own government must have a beginning and an end of its years. These days are marked, for the citizens, in different ways. We have, as I said, the Fourth of July, the birthday of America's independence, and Dominion Day in Canada. We have the first Tuesday after the first Monday in November, which is election day. We have the 20th of January, which is inauguration day every four years. For your parents—a big day is April 15th, when they have to pay taxes. In olden times, too, kings marked the beginning of their reign, and they had an official birthday. So far as Mishnah is concerned, that birthday is the beginning of the month of spring, Nisan.

That is the time, in the Land of Israel, when the new year begins in another, more important way, mentioned at the beginning of our Mishnah: the *festivals*.

What festival takes place in Nisan? Passover, of course. We begin the cycle of the three festivals then. Passover is followed, seven weeks later, by Shabu'ot (Weeks). In the fall, at the end of the summer dryness and at the beginning of the fall rains, comes Sukkot, the most important festival of all.

So Nisan marks the beginning of two important cycles of the year: the cycle of government and the cycle of the festivals.

II. *Elul*

Elul generally corresponds to August and is the new year for giving the tithe of animals. To understand this rule, we have to go back to the written Torah. In Leviticus 27:32, we find the following:

> And all the tithe of herds and flocks, every tenth animal of all that
> pass under the herdsman's staff, shall be holy to the Lord.

This law means God owns one out of every ten animals born in a given year. It is the least we owe to God who creates the things that sustain our lives. We measure the end of one year and the beginning of the next—for the purpose of knowing which animals are owed to God—on the first of Elul. This, of course, is not part of our own lives. But there is a corresponding new year.

Every year the Jewish community of your town or city raises money for holy purposes: to help poor people, to support Jewish schools, to take care of Jews who need help in other parts of the world and to help build the State of Israel. That "time of giving" is not through the year. There is a particular part of the year, a period of a few months, when people work hard to raise money for Jewish causes. It is called "the campaign," and it is the work of ordinary Jewish people—like you and me—who join together in a "Jewish Federation" or "Jewish Welfare Fund."

In most communities, the time for giving to the holy cause of the Jewish people is very special. Much other work stops for that time, so that everyone can concentrate on this most important job. When is the Jewish community drive for money held in your community? Sometimes it is in the spring, and in other communities it is in the fall. This is the Jewish people's new year for charity. It corresponds to the new year marked by Elul.

III. *Tishré*

Here we have many new years:

1. the beginning of years;

2. the new year for the year of release (which I'll explain in half a minute);

3. the new year for the jubilee (I'll explain that one too);

4. the new year for the planting of trees (and if you think you know what this is, you might be wrong);

5. and the new year for vegetables (ditto).

Tishré is generally the month that corresponds to September. What are Mishnah's new years for Tishré?

1. *The beginning of years.* This is obvious. You know that we count the Jewish years from the first day of Tishré, what we know as Rosh Hashshanah. This day is similar to the first day of January of the secular year. That's an easy one. But you notice that Mishnah doesn't tell us why this matters. That's because Mishnah here is just giving us a catalogue.

2. *The year of release and the jubilee:* Once again we have to open our written Torah. This time we turn to Leviticus 25:1-4:

> The Lord said to Moses on Mount Sinai, "Say to the people of Israel: When you come into the land which I give you, the land shall keep a sabbath to the Lord. Six years you shall sow your field, and six years you shall prune your vineyard, and gather in its fruits. But in the seventh year there shall be a sabbath of solemn rest for the land, a Sabbath to the Lord. You shall not sow your field or prune your vineyard.

This seventh year is a sign that God owns the land, and we are God's tenants. Nothing we have belongs entirely to us.

That is the same point, of course, that we just made about the kind of property represented by cattle. In our time, the equivalent might be a machine that helps us make our living and belongs to our employer. Part of what you make on the machine belongs to the one who owns the machine.

But the main point is simple. We must never think that the things we enjoy really belong to us. They are gifts to us, for which we must be grateful. We cannot take them for granted. The land that God gives to the people of Israel is God's land. By letting the land enjoy a Sabbath every seven years, just as we enjoy a Sabbath every seven days, we indicate that the land is like us: It serves, but it also rests, just as we work but also rest. Once in seven years, we don't do anything to make the land serve us. This is the sign that the land belongs to God. We don't plough the land or till it or plant seeds and harvest the crops. The land lies fallow. That is the meaning of the seventh year, the year of release, which as we know, begins on the first day of Tishré.

The jubilee year is easy to explain once you understand the sabbatical year. Leviticus 25:8-13 says:

> And you shall count seven weeks of years, seven times seven years, so that the time of the seven weeks of years shall be to you forty-nine years. Then you shall send abroad the loud trumpet on the tenth day of the seventh month; on the day of atonement you shall send abroad the trumpet throughout all your land. And you shall make holy the fiftieth year and proclaim liberty throughout the land to all its inhabitants. It shall be a jubilee for you, when each of you shall return to his property and each of you shall return to his family. A jubilee shall that fiftieth year be to you.

What a deep idea—after forty-nine years there is the fiftieth year celebrated as a jubilee—a completely new beginning for everyone's life. Everyone is freed from the slavery of the past. Everyone is free to return home again. It would take us a long time to appreciate the full depth and significance of this idea. For our present purpose, it is enough to note that, as far as Mishnah is concerned, the jubilee year begins also on the first day of Tishré. But there is more for Tishré—what a new year!

There is also the new year for trees. The rule here is that when we plant a tree, we cannot eat its fruit for the first three years. At whatever time in the year we plant the tree—it may be in April or in June—we count the year's passing at Tishré, so that the second year begins at the rosh hashshanah for fruit-trees.

And the point about vegetables is just as obvious. We have to give, to holy purposes, ten percent of the vegetables we grow. But, as in the case of cattle, we give tithe for vegetables that we pick within a given year. We don't mix up vegetables that we pick the year earlier or the year later. The first of Tishré marks the end of one year of harvesting. Whatever is picked in the preceding year has to be kept separate and tithed separately from what is picked in the next year.

This has been a complicated story. What is the main point in all this? We answer that question in a moment. We're almost finished with this interesting, but hard, Mishnah.

IV. *Shebat*

This one is easy. On the first of Shebat (the House of Shammai say) or on the fifteenth of Shebat (the House of Hillel say) we mark the new year for trees. You know that the House of Hillel's date is the right one, because on the fifteenth of Shebat (Tu biShebat) we observe the new year of the trees. In the land of Israel they plant trees on that date. In many parts of North America it is cold and snowy on that day. We can't plant trees. But we do eat fruit in honor of the day.

The meaning of Mishnah is somewhat different. It is the same meaning as we have seen before. On the first (or fifteenth) of Shebat we mark the birthday of the trees. Trees' fruits have to be tithed year by year. We separate fruit that has ripened in the year before Shebat from fruit that will ripen in the next year. We give tithe from the fruit of the former year separately from the tithe we give from the fruit of the latter. By now this is a familiar idea.

WHAT IS THE POINT?

First, we notice that Mishnah does not want us to mix up the affairs of one year with those of the next. It takes seriously the notion of a *new* year. If we have to give a portion of our possessions to the purposes of the Lord, we don't give a mixture of one thing and another. What comes into our hand in one year is kept separate from what comes into our hand in the next. If you paid taxes, you'd know that our government has the same view. There is a beginning and an end to everything.

WHAT DOES IT MEAN TO ME?

Things end, and things begin. What you do this year can stop. You can make a new beginning in your life and have a fresh start.

Young children know this. They think that on their birthday something important happens, something changes. They no longer are five-year-olds. Now they're six-year-olds.

You are not too old to have forgotten this. But what does it mean to you? It means the same thing: when you're thirteen you're no longer twelve, and you're not yet fourteen. A birthday means a change. It means a chance for a fresh start. A new year—whether it is your new year, your school's new year, the new year of your family, the new year of your synagogue or the new year of your Jewish community—means something truly important: a new opportunity.

Life renews itself constantly, every day. That is not as big and general an idea as it seems. Bring it down into your own life, your own school, your own family, your own community. We always have another chance, a new chance. That is Mishnah's deep and important message, and that is why I thought it important enough to spend all this time and effort learning the details of a long-ago new year, an olden calendar.

It should be easy for you to make a Mishnah like this Mishnah. But it should not be too easy. We want to find out different new years—a new year for yourself, your birthday, your school, the beginning of classes and the move from one grade to the next. We *also* want to find out different *kinds* of new years—new years which are going to mark new beginnings for quite different things.

1. **Why is a birthday important?**
2. **What do we mean by a fresh start? Why does a new year mark a chance for a new beginning?**
3. **What is Rosh Hashshanah as we know it? What do we celebrate on that day? What do people say about the familiar Rosh Hashshanah?**
4. **Why do parents celebrate their wedding anniversary? What other anniversaries do you celebrate in your family?**

5. What are the sorts of things Mishnah lists when it tells us about new years? Are they all alike? Or are they different new years for different kinds of things entirely? You recall from Sesame Street, One of these things is not like the other. Try to figure out what sorts of new years cover the same sort of thing, and what sorts of new years mark quite different things—for instance—new years for nature, new years for people, new years for government, and so on.

6. Why is the new year for the Jewish community—its time of giving for holy Jewish causes—the most important new year today? Why do Jewish people think it important to set aside a time to collect the money they must have? How does that new year enter into your life?

7. Why do we celebrate the new year of the trees differently from the way it is celebrated in the Land of Israel?

8. Why is it important to have another chance?

What A Day!

MISHNAH YOMA 8:9

ishnah speaks about new years we've never heard of. It also speaks about the holiest day of the year—Yom Kippur—of which we have heard. And it says something important about that day. What differences does a day make? It can make all the difference in the world—if it's a *certain* day.

A day marks a change in life. You already know that. But so far, we've looked at the difference a day can make only from one viewpoint. A day *marks* a change. A day signifies the movement from one thing to another—from being eleven to being twelve. But the day doesn't really *do* anything. It simply sits there. *On* it something happens.

But that's only one kind of special day. The other kind is really special because the day itself *makes* the difference—the day, and what you do on it, and only on that particular day.

There's a birthday. There's the day you become a *bar misvah* or *bat misvah*. There's new year, January 1, when you change the date on your calendar. And then there's Rosh Hashshanah, when you spend much time in *tefillot* and think about yourself and who you are. But then there's still another day—a day which Torah teaches has its *own* power. It's not only what you do on that day, but all the more so what that day itself may mean. The day itself has its own weight, its own force, a kind of power of its own.

And there's only one such day—Yom Kippur. What is the power of Yom Kippur? The oral Torah wants to ask exactly that question. We know the answer: it's in the name of the day itself, the day of covering over or forgiving.

The oral Torah sees Yom Kippur as a day that, all by itself, has the power to bring forgiveness for the sins we've done. What an amazing idea! A day that, all by itself, can go up before God and beg for forgiveness for the peoples' sins. A day that is a kind of person, not merely the time between sunset and sunset. Yom Kippur is a day that is able to do things by itself.

Yom Kippur is the day that has that power by its very being to rise to

God and say, "Forgive your children, who make mistakes."

That idea is amazing, beautiful and true. It also is dangerous. If you believe that something can gain forgiveness for you, then why not say, "Fine, I'll do anything I want because Yom Kippur will make things right."

That is not how it works. The oral Torah is far too interested in you, in your attitudes and your intentions to let you get off that easily. The Mishnah before us talks about plain things in an open and obvious way. This is how it goes.

MISHNAH YOMA 8:9

הָאוֹמֵר: אֶחֱטָא וְאָשׁוּב, אֶחֱטָא וְאָשׁוּב — אֵין מַסְפִּיקִין בְּיָדוֹ לַעֲשׂוֹת תְּשׁוּבָה; אֶחֱטָא, וְיוֹם הַכִּפּוּרִים מְכַפֵּר — אֵין יוֹם הַכִּפּוּרִים מְכַפֵּר. עֲבֵרוֹת שֶׁבֵּין אָדָם לַמָּקוֹם — יוֹם הַכִּפּוּרִים מְכַפֵּר; עֲבֵרוֹת שֶׁבֵּין אָדָם לַחֲבֵרוֹ — אֵין יוֹם הַכִּפּוּרִים מְכַפֵּר, עַד שֶׁיְּרַצֶּה אֶת חֲבֵרוֹ. אֶת זוֹ דָרַשׁ רַבִּי אֶלְעָזָר בֶּן עֲזַרְיָה: 'מִכֹּל חַטֹּאתֵיכֶם לִפְנֵי ה' תִּטְהָרוּ'; עֲבֵרוֹת שֶׁבֵּין אָדָם לַמָּקוֹם — יוֹם הַכִּפּוּרִים מְכַפֵּר; עֲבֵרוֹת שֶׁבֵּין אָדָם לַחֲבֵרוֹ — אֵין יוֹם הַכִּפּוּרִים מְכַפֵּר, עַד שֶׁיְּרַצֶּה אֶת חֲבֵרוֹ. אָמַר רַבִּי עֲקִיבָא: אַשְׁרֵיכֶם יִשְׂרָאֵל! לִפְנֵי מִי אַתֶּם מְטַהֲרִין? מִי מְטַהֵר אֶתְכֶם? אֲבִיכֶם שֶׁבַּשָּׁמַיִם, שֶׁנֶּאֱמַר: 'וְזָרַקְתִּי עֲלֵיכֶם מַיִם טְהוֹרִים וּטְהַרְתֶּם'; וְאוֹמֵר: 'מִקְוֵה יִשְׂרָאֵל ה'', מָה הַמִּקְוֶה מְטַהֵר אֶת הַטְּמֵאִים, אַף הַקָּדוֹשׁ בָּרוּךְ הוּא מְטַהֵר אֶת יִשְׂרָאֵל.

Vocabulary

he who says	הָאוֹמֵר	to do	לַעֲשׂוֹת
I will sin	אֶחֱטָא	repentance	תְּשׁוּבָה
I will repent	אָשׁוּב	Yom Kippur	יוֹם הַכִּפּוּרִים
there is no	אֵין	effect atonement	מְכַפֵּר
opportunity	מַסְפִּיקִין	transgressions	עֲבֵרוֹת
for him	בְּיָדוֹ	between	בֵּין

86

man	אָדָם	·	your Father	אֲבִיכֶם
The Lord	מָקוֹם		in heaven	בַּשָּׁמַיִם
his fellow	חֲבֵרוֹ		as it is written	שֶׁנֶּאֱמַר
until	עַד		I will sprinkle	וְזָרַקְתִּי
he appeases	יְרַצֶּה		on you	עֲלֵיכֶם
expound	דָּרַשׁ		water	מַיִם
your sins	חַטֹּאתֵיכֶם		hope	מִקְוֶה
before	לִפְנֵי		the immersion-pool	הַמִּקְוֶה
you will be clean	תִּטְהָרוּ		the unclean	הַטְּמֵאִים
you are happy	אַשְׁרֵיכֶם			

HOW THE MISHNAH WORKS

The first thing we have to do, as usual, is take apart the Mishnah into its pieces and see how it works. It's long and also a mixture of several separate parts. Here is the first part.

How the Mishnah Is Put Together

He who says	1 הָאוֹמֵר:
I shall sin and repent, sin and repent	אֶחֱטָא וְאָשׁוּב, אֶחֱטָא וְאָשׁוּב —
there is no opportunity for him to do repentance.	אֵין מַסְפִּיקִין בְּיָדוֹ לַעֲשׂוֹת תְּשׁוּבָה;
(He who says), I shall sin, and the Day of Atonement will atone	אֶחֱטָא, וְיוֹם הַכִּפּוּרִים מְכַפֵּר —
the Day of Atonement does not atone.	אֵין יוֹם הַכִּפּוּרִים מְכַפֵּר.

87

Sins which are between man and the Omnipresent	2 עֲבֵרוֹת שֶׁבֵּין אָדָם לַמָּקוֹם —
the Day of Atonement atones for.	יוֹם הַכִּפּוּרִים מְכַפֵּר;
Sins which are between man and his fellow	עֲבֵרוֹת שֶׁבֵּין אָדָם לַחֲבֵרוֹ —
the Day of Atonement does not atone for	אֵין יוֹם הַכִּפּוּרִים מְכַפֵּר,
until one will win the good will of his fellow (once more).	עַד שֶׁיְּרַצֶּה אֶת חֲבֵרוֹ.
This is what Rabbi Eleazar ben 'Azariah expounded:	3 אֶת זוֹ דָרַשׁ רַבִּי אֶלְעָזָר בֶּן עֲזַרְיָה:
From all your sins shall you be clean before the Lord (Lev. 16:30)	'מִכֹּל חַטֹּאתֵיכֶם לִפְנֵי ה' תִּטְהָרוּ';
Sins which are between man and the Omnipresent	עֲבֵרוֹת שֶׁבֵּין אָדָם לַמָּקוֹם —
the Day of Atonement atones for.	יוֹם הַכִּפּוּרִים מְכַפֵּר;
Sins which are between man and his fellow	עֲבֵרוֹת שֶׁבֵּין אָדָם לַחֲבֵרוֹ —
the Day of Atonement does not atone for	אֵין יוֹם הַכִּפּוּרִים מְכַפֵּר,
until one will win the good will of his fellow.	עַד שֶׁיְּרַצֶּה אֶת חֲבֵרוֹ.

 e see that we have quite a construction before us. It's not going to be easy to memorize because it is long and not tight or well balanced. But you can certainly learn the first three parts without much difficulty because each is a little couplet.

The first stands all by itself. It says the same thing twice. If you say, "I'll sin and then say I'm sorry," you can never say you're sorry enough. Saying you're sorry is not possible if you did something deliberately and maliciously. That, as I said, is all by itself. The same exact thought is repeated in No. 2 and No. 3. The same words are used in both.

But No. 3 attaches the words to a particular name and to a particular verse in the written Torah, and No. 2 just gives us the gist of the idea all by itself. That's why it's easy to remember Nos. 2 and 3.

Then, as we'll see in a moment, comes 'Aqiva in No. 4. And he stands all by himself, and he says something new. He says it twice—the same thought in two versions. Both require a verse to prove that what he says is right.

Now let's turn to what the people say about Yom Kippur.

"I'LL SIN AND SAY I'M SORRY"

That doesn't go. You have to *mean* you're sorry and that you wouldn't have done what you did if you'd known it was wrong. We just saw this in the last lesson. How can you be sorry about something you *meant* to do to begin with? If you say, "I'll do something bad and then say I'm sorry," that doesn't matter. You can never really say you're sorry and be believed.

The same thing applies to Yom Kippur. If you say, "I'll do whatever I want to because when Yom Kippur comes, it will make things right"—that doesn't help one bit. Yom Kippur won't help you. It won't work at all.

Because—like everything else in the oral Torah—your own attitude is the most important thing and decides everything else. If you have the wrong attitude to begin with, then there's no magic in the world that will help. There's only the magic of your *own* will and intention.

And what that means is that you are the most important and most powerful thing in the world. You decide what really matters and what really works. If you have the right attitude, everything works. But if you have the wrong attitude, nothing is sufficiently powerful to work at all.

That goes for Yom Kippur, that awesome day! You fast all day, you pray, you spend the day in a serious mood, and you pass much of the day—or all day long—in the synagogue. If you don't have the right attitude, this doesn't work, it doesn't even matter. If you say, "I'll do anything and let Yom Kippur settle matters," that's hopeless!

·

WELL, YOM KIPPUR CAN HELP

No, it can't—not all by itself. Yom Kippur works only when it has to do with God. But your attitude and your actions with other people in this world make Yom Kippur work, or make it impossible for Yom Kippur to work.

No. 2 and No. 3 tell us that there are two kinds of sins. There are sins that have to do with God alone—which don't do harm to any person—like vowing or swearing. And there are sins—which are common and which we can list—that have to do with other people. You hurt someone's feelings. You break a promise to someone. You hit someone for no reason.

Yom Kippur won't help you. It's true that when you hurt someone else you sin against God too. But God takes second place. First of all, you have to say you're sorry to the person you've hurt. Then you have to say you're sorry to God. If you pray all day long—but you haven't made peace with your friend—all your prayers go up like smoke.

The oral Torah tells us that Yom Kippur doesn't work until you *make* it work. You make it work by setting things right with the people you've wronged. Only then does the great day do its great thing.

So these five lines, the first four matching, come to a climax in the fifth: *Until you make peace with your fellow.* Everything leads to that one important thought.

Said Rabbi 'Aqiva:	אָמַר רַבִּי עֲקִיבָא:
Happy are you, O Israel!	אַשְׁרֵיכֶם יִשְׂרָאֵל!
Before whom are you purified?	לִפְנֵי מִי אַתֶּם מְטַהֲרִין?
Who purifies you?	מִי מְטַהֵר אֶתְכֶם?
Your Father who is in heaven.	אֲבִיכֶם שֶׁבַּשָּׁמַיִם,
As it is said, And I will sprinkle clean water on you and you will be clean (Ezekiel 36:25).	שֶׁנֶּאֱמַר: 'וְזָרַקְתִּי עֲלֵיכֶם מַיִם טְהוֹרִים וּטְהַרְתֶּם';
And it says, The hope of Israel is the Lord (Jeremiah 17:13).	וְאוֹמֵר: 'מִקְוֵה יִשְׂרָאֵל ה'' ';
Just as the immersion-pool cleans the unclean people,	מָה הַמִּקְוֶה מְטַהֵר אֶת הַטְּמֵאִים,
So the Holy One, blessed be he, cleans Israel.	אַף הַקָּדוֹשׁ בָּרוּךְ הוּא מְטַהֵר אֶת יִשְׂרָאֵל.

qiva comes along with his own thought. He, of course, agrees with what has been said before. But he wants to say something new. His message is this: We should be happy when we consider who cares for us, who makes us clean of sin. Israel—the Jewish people—is like a child who plays in the mud all day. In the evening the child comes home. Does the parent say, "You're all dirty! Go somewhere else! I don't want to see you!" No, the parent doesn't say that. The parent says, "Come on in. I'll give you a bath. I'll make you clean again." And that's God and Israel. Israel wallows in the mud all day, all year. It gets dirty. It does many bad things. And the mud has to be washed off because Israel can't do it all by itself. So what happens?

On Yom Kippur, Israel—all the Jews in the world —come before God. And they're all dirty and can't wash off the dirt. And God says, "I'll splash nice warm water on you and wash off the mud." And then comes the play on words: *miqveh* meaning *hope*, and *miqveh* meaning a nice clean warm *bath*. God is Israel's *hope*—because God is Israel's *soap*.

We don't get discouraged, give up and say, "I'm just hopeless! I'm so dirty, I'm so filthy, no one can do any good for me. I might as well stay this way and wallow around in the mud." We hope that there's someone who can clean us up. And so we want to be clean even though we're dirty. God gives us hope—because God cleans us up—on Yom Kippur.

That's the whole message. We do something for ourselves because if we don't make peace with other people, nothing will help. But God is still there to clean us up.

WHAT DOES IT MEAN TO ME?

We've talked about two things: 1. the power of a day and 2. the power of our own attitude. They're things you can't touch or feel. But they're powerful. Just as your own attitude shapes the things you do, so a day can shape the year. Just as what you *mean* can make the same word good or bad, so what you do on a certain day can make that day important or trivial.

But the main thing we've talked about is something we haven't even mentioned until now: *What you think about yourself.*

The most important thing is whether or not you like yourself. If you don't, you won't like anyone else, and if you do, you will like everyone else, too. Whether or not you like yourself depends upon whether you think that you are a good person, or whether you go around feeling ashamed of yourself, sorry for things you've done and worried about things you're going to do.

It's natural to feel sorry for something you've done and ashamed of something you've said. But it's not natural to feel that you're ruined forever.

You can't carry that burden, that heavy load of shame. At some point something has to take that pack off your back and say, "Fine, it's too bad. But let's stand up straight and take a walk down a new path."

That's what Yom Kippur does for us. But it doesn't do it automatically. It doesn't happen by magic. What we do wrong is to other people, and we feel ashamed of ourselves because of things we've said or done to other people. So we start by taking off the weight we put on our own back. And then Yom Kippur helps us stand up straight and take that first step down a new path.

This is the heart and soul of Mishnah. It applies, to the most private and secret parts of our life, that same truth that it applies to the public and open parts of our life: everything depends on your own attitude, on your own *will*.

1. What difference has a single day made in your own life? Can you think of a day which changed everything, whether to the good or otherwise? What day was so important that everything afterward was different from everything be-fore-hand?
2. What are "sins between man and God"?
3. What are "sins between man and man"?
4. Why should God care about your making peace with your friend before you come for forgiveness to God? Why is this the most important part of Yom Kippur?
5. Why does 'Aqiva say Israel is happy? What is his opinion of the idea of Eleazar ben 'Azariah? Does he agree with Eleazar? Does Eleazar agree with 'Aqiva?
6. People fast on Yom Kippur. Why do they do so? What difference does that make? It this part of "making Yom Kippur work"?
7. Why is your own attitude the most important thing of all? How does our Mishnah try to express that very idea? Is it really true that your own attitude decides everything else?

Thanks a Lot! For What?

MISHNAH BERAKHOT 6:1-2

You want to do the right thing in the right way. If you give a friend a birthday present—but you just throw it at him or her and don't say, "Happy birthday"—it isn't much of a present. If someone gives you a stick of gum, and you say, "Thanks. You saved my life. I'll love you forever," that too is the wrong way of saying thanks. The first way is too little, the second way, too much.

When it comes to thanking God, we surely need help to do it correctly. After all, when and how could we find a way *not* to say thanks to God who made the world and who created us? Everything we have and love—everything we are—we owe to God. So we could decide to spend every minute of every day mumbling thanks for this and thanks for that, and that would not be realistic. It would turn our natural and real feelings of gratitude into a burden, into something we wish we didn't have to bear.

So one of the things Mishnah tells us is 1. how to thank God and 2. for what to thank God. This lesson and the next deal with two different things for which we thank God, and they tell us what to say. For just as important as it is to know *that* we should say thanks, it is also important to know *how* to say thanks.

The way we say thanks is through a blessing said over certain things. The most important blessing is for food. And what we say over food is interesting.

We don't say that God went out into the field and planted seeds, tended the shoots and harvested the crops, made the crops into food we can eat, brought it to the supermarket, went to the store and bought it, prepared it, put it onto plates and served it to us. We don't say that because it isn't true. Many different people have to work long and hard to make the food we eat: the farmer, the trucker, the processor, and, finally, our mothers and fathers who get the food and prepare it for us to eat.

Yet we do think that somewhere along the line all of these things happen because God makes them happen. How many thousands of words should we need to list all the things God does so that all the people can do the things that, in the end, put food on our plates! Mishnah doesn't think you need thousands of words. All Mishnah wants you to do is say, in two or three words, just what it is that God does. And it uses words that cover everything.

These words just *describe* those long and hard processes that put food on our plates. They say God *creates* this thing or that thing. That is, a blessing is a way of saying we know something—a way of *acknowledging* something. That whatever happens, God makes it happen.

When we say a blessing over bread, all we say is that it is God who—through all the different acts of labor of different people—is the One who brings forth bread from the ground.

Now a loaf of bread doesn't come from the ground. Little shoots of wheat come up, and then there are many processes by which the shoots of wheat are turned into pieces of bread for us to eat. God is behind all this. When we say a blessing, we say just that: God brings forth bread from the ground, God creates fruit of fruit-trees, God creates the produce of the ground, God makes all these things.

That's all we have to say. But it's enough. We simply say we *acknowledge*—we know, and we're thankful. What God does, God does through people. And all these people do what they do so that, in the end, we eat. That's what we're thankful for when we say a blessing.

When you learn Mishnah, you learn how you should act. If you *do* those things, they change you. You become someone more alert and aware of things that you didn't do before and that you do now. This is Mishnah's goal—to make you into a person who thinks before doing, who asks questions about matters other people take for granted. If your friend gives you a piece of gum, you say thanks. If your mother picks you up from school on a rainy day, you say thanks. If your teacher says you wrote a good paper, you say thanks. If you're on third base with two outs, and someone hits a single and you score, you say thanks. If you have a big birthday party, you say thanks.

That doesn't make total sense. It doesn't really say it. Because you enjoy many kinds of gifts and have to say thanks—because you really want to—for many kinds of things.

The same thanks you say for a piece of gum hardly covers the gratitude you feel when you think of all the things your mother and father do for you. And the appreciation you feel to them is different from the gratitude you feel to your teammate who scores the winning run. In a way, you have to make a mixture of *thanks* and *thinks*. You want to learn to think about thanks, to learn that there are many things people do for you, and to figure out how to express yourself in an appropriate way.

The Mishnah paragraphs before us teach two lessons. 1. That we have to find a way of giving thanks for different things and 2. exactly what we are supposed to do, in particular, to thank God for things God does for us and gives to us.

Mishnah is not generalities. Mishnah talks about specific things in specific ways. It's not "piety," ideas no one can carry out in everyday life. Mishnah talks about the concrete and specific things of here and now.

MISHNAH BERAKHOT 6:1-2

כֵּיצַד מְבָרְכִין עַל הַפֵּרוֹת? עַל פֵּרוֹת הָאִילָן הוּא אוֹמֵר 'בּוֹרֵא פְּרִי הָעֵץ', חוּץ מִן הַיַּיִן, שֶׁעַל הַיַּיִן הוּא אוֹמֵר 'בּוֹרֵא פְּרִי הַגָּפֶן'. וְעַל פֵּרוֹת הָאָרֶץ הוּא אוֹמֵר 'בּוֹרֵא פְּרִי הָאֲדָמָה', חוּץ מִן הַפַּת, שֶׁעַל הַפַּת הוּא אוֹמֵר 'הַמּוֹצִיא לֶחֶם מִן הָאָרֶץ'. וְעַל הַיְרָקוֹת הוּא אוֹמֵר 'בּוֹרֵא פְּרִי הָאֲדָמָה'. רַבִּי יְהוּדָה אוֹמֵר 'בּוֹרֵא מִינֵי דְשָׁאִים'.   בֵּרַךְ עַל פֵּרוֹת הָאִילָן 'בּוֹרֵא פְּרִי הָאֲדָמָה', יָצָא; וְעַל פֵּרוֹת הָאָרֶץ 'בּוֹרֵא פְּרִי הָעֵץ', לֹא יָצָא. עַל כֻּלָּם — אִם אָמַר 'שֶׁהַכֹּל נִהְיָה בִדְבָרוֹ', יָצָא.

Vocabulary

how	כֵּיצַד	creates	בּוֹרֵא
bless	מְבָרְכִין	tree	עֵץ
on, for	עַל	except	חוּץ
pieces of fruit	פֵּרוֹת	for, from	מִן
tree	אִילָן	wine	יַיִן

vine	גֶּפֶן	kinds of seed	מִינֵי דְשָׁאִים
the land	הָאָרֶץ	do one's duty	יָצָא
ground	אֲדָמָה	all of them	כֻּלָּם
piece of bread	פַּת	if	אִם
brings out	מוֹצִיא	everything	הַכֹּל
bread	לֶחֶם	come into being	נִהְיָה
vegetables	יְרָקוֹת	his word	דְּבָרוֹ

How the Mishnah Is Put Together

How do they say a blessing over fruit?	כֵּיצַד מְבָרְכִין עַל הַפֵּרוֹת?	1
Over fruit of a tree, a person says.	עַל פֵּרוֹת הָאִילָן הוּא אוֹמֵר	2
(Blessed are you, Lord our God, ruler of the world, who) creates fruit of the tree.	'בּוֹרֵא פְּרִי הָעֵץ',	
Except for wine, for	חוּץ מִן הַיַּיִן,	3
over wine, a person says,	שֶׁעַל הַיַּיִן הוּא אוֹמֵר	4
(Blessed are you, Lord, our God, ruler of the world, who) creates fruit of the vine.	'בּוֹרֵא פְּרִי הַגֶּפֶן'.	
And over fruit of the ground a person says,	וְעַל פֵּרוֹת הָאָרֶץ הוּא אוֹמֵר	5
(Blessed are you, Lord, our God, ruler of the world, who) creates fruit of the ground.	'בּוֹרֵא פְּרִי הָאֲדָמָה',	
Except for bread, for	חוּץ מִן הַפַּת,	6

over bread, a person says,

(Blessed are you, Lord, our God, ruler of the world) who brings bread out of the earth.

And over vegetables, a person says,

(Blessed are you, Lord, our God, ruler of the world, who) creates fruit of the ground.

Rabbi Judah says,

(A person says, Blessed are you, Lord our God, ruler of the world, who) creates different kinds of seeds.

7 שֶׁעַל הַפַּת הוּא אוֹמֵר
'הַמּוֹצִיא לֶחֶם מִן הָאָרֶץ'.

8 וְעַל הַיְרָקוֹת הוּא אוֹמֵר
'בּוֹרֵא פְּרִי הָאֲדָמָה'.

9 רַבִּי יְהוּדָה אוֹמֵר
'בּוֹרֵא מִינֵי דְשָׁאִים'.

The first thing you notice, once again, is that we have taken the Mishnah apart. Each thought is given separately. We see that the first six lines (Nos. 1-7) are a little poem that begins with a question. Sets of matching sentences (nos. 2, 3, 4 and 5, 6, 7) answer. Thus we see:

1
2,3,4
5,6,7

And at each point, there is a match.

It's easy to remember this Mishnah because all you have to do is remember that you have four categories, two by two: 1. fruit of trees, 2. except for wine, 3. fruit of the ground, 4. except for bread. Nothing could be easier. Obviously, you'll know the question—how do they bless? Remembering the answer is the main challenge. And that is as easy as memorizing a little poem.

Nos. 8 and 9 are a separate unit. They, too, are easy to remember. First, you notice that No. 3 is arranged the same as Nos. 2, 4, 5, and 7. So, in point of fact, we have three categories in all:

1. Fruit of trees
2. Fruit of ground
3. Vegetables

Second, you notice a disagreement. Judah has a different opinion. He does cite a blessing. This brings us to the actual rules.

Clearly, there are different blessings for different things. Each thing has to have the correct blessing. (In a minute, we're going to see that that isn't really so.)

First, let's consider the different blessings, and then we'll talk about why there are different ones. In all, how many different blessings are in our Mishnah?

I count the ones in Nos. 2, 4, 5, 7, 8 and 9—six are specified. But, of course, the blessing in No. 5 and the one in No. 8 are the same. So someone has given them separately in order to make a poem with nine units, another multiple of threes.

What are the blessings? Let's learn them.

FOR FRUIT OF THE TREE

What fruits grow on trees? How many can you list? We say:

Blessed are you, Lord, our God, ruler of the whole world, who creates fruit of trees.

FOR WINE

Wine is special. In the land of Israel it is one of the most important things produced by farming. It has its own blessing:

Blessed are you, Lord, our God, ruler of the whole world who creates the fruit of the vine.

FOR THINGS WHICH GROW IN THE GROUND

What things grow in the ground? How many can you list? The blessing is:

Blessed are you, Lord, our God, ruler of the whole world, who creates fruit of the earth.

FOR BREAD

Bread is special too because long ago in the Land of Israel, bread was the main food that people ate. Everything else was secondary. So bread had its own blessing. The blessing is:

Blessed are you, Lord, our God, ruler of the whole world, who brings out bread from the earth.

Notice that here we don't use the word 'creates,' as we do in all the other blessings. We are more specific.

FOR VEGETABLES

Vegetables don't grow in the earth. They grow from plants that grow in the earth. What vegetables are in this category? The blessing is:

Blessed are you, Lord, our God, ruler of the whole world who creates the fruit of the ground.

Judah has a different view, but it's not very different. He wants to refer to different kinds of seeds.

What do we notice about Mishnah as a whole? It is obvious that Mishnah does not tell us the complete blessing. Mishnah tells us only the crucial words. Mishnah assumes we know something that it does not have to spell out:

1. We know what a blessing is.
2. We know why we are supposed to say blessings.

3. We know the different blessings we might say.

4. We know the formula that is shared by all these blessings.

5. And we need only to know which one we use for which food.

Yet, once you give these answers, why should there be any question?
Look again:

> How do they bless fruit?
> For fruit of the tree one says,
> Who creates fruit of the tree.

What should you say? What would you expect? Fruit of the *ground?* Nonsense. As soon as you ask the question, "How do they bless different kinds of fruit?" And then you specify, fruit of the *tree*—you know the answer!

So Mishnah is not really what it seems to be. It teaches something we already know. But it nonetheless teaches. What Mishnah wants to do is to tell us what we know and what we can figure out—if we know Mishnah! That is why we memorize it. What is important in Mishnah is that we know it. Once we know it, we automatically can make sense of it.

Is Mishnah trying to give us information? No. It assumes we already have information. Mishnah tries to make use of information we already have. This Mishnah of ours is strange. Now you know why I told you, "You don't just reach Mishnah, you *learn* it." This brings us to the second Mishnah, the neighbor and friend of the one we have just studied. I haven't forgotten that we want to know how Mishnah is relevant to our circumstances. That will come in a moment. First, let's take the Mishnah apart and see how it is put together.

MISHNAH BERAKHOT 6:2

(If) a person said a blessing over fruits of the tree,	1 בֵּרַךְ עַל פֵּרוֹת הָאִילָן
"Who creates the fruit of the ground"	'בּוֹרֵא פְּרִי הָאֲדָמָה',
he has carried out his obligation	יָצָא;
And (if he said a blessing) over fruits of the ground,	2 וְעַל פֵּרוֹת הָאָרֶץ

101

"Who creates the fruit of the
tree"

'בּוֹרֵא פְּרִי הָעֵץ',

he has not carried out his
obligation.

לֹא יָצָא.

And for all of them, if he
said,

4 עַל כֻּלָּם — אִם אָמַר

(Blessed are you, Lord our
God, ruler of the world)
by whose word all things
come into being

'שֶׁהַכֹּל נִהְיָה בִּדְבָרוֹ',

he has carried out his
obligation

יָצָא.

s before, we have a little
poem which is, naturally, in
three parts. No. 1 and No. 2
match. The second part
needs the verb of the first
part, *blessed*. Otherwise they
are identical: "If I said over X,
blessing Y, I have carried out
my obligation. If I said over Y
blessing X, I have *not* carried
out my obligation." We'll ask why in a moment. Let's keep our attention
fixed on our poem.

No. 3 winds up everything. After all the work we've been through to
learn all the different blessings for different things, how do we come out?
There is a single blessing that is all right for everything!

What is the point? What happens if I say a blessing for fruit of the
ground, but I say it for fruit of trees? That's all right. Why? Because, after all,
trees grow from the ground. They are not so different from those vegetables
that draw nourishment from the ground. But what happens if I say a blessing
for fruit of trees, but I say it for fruit of the ground? That's *not* all right. Why

not? Because I haven't really said the right thing for the fruit of the ground. They don't come from trees.

The most important thought comes at the end. True, we should say the specific blessing for the right food. But there is a blessing that covers all food. And what is it? It is a blessing that makes the point clear:

> *Blessed are you, Lord, our God, ruler of the whole world by whose word all things come into being.*

What could be simpler? What could cover more things? For God makes everything, brings everything into being. That simple blessing, therefore, is suitable for everything.

WHAT DOES IT MEAN TO ME?

We have worked hard to understand exactly what Mishnah says and the words Mishnah uses to say what it wants to say. What have we learned from all this?

First, we now know that you have to say thanks in one way for one thing, in another way for another. That means that we think *about* the different things people give us, the different things God gives us. And that means, above all, that we *think*. We don't take anything for granted. There is always something to think about. Thanking requires thinking. Everything requires thinking.

Second, we have learned the specific blessings that we're supposed to say for different foods. But we've also found out that there is one blessing that says something so important, that it says it all: *Everything comes into being because of God's word.* That is the thought that all of these blessings try to put into our minds.

But that means, too, that we have to balance between doing the right thing in the right way, on the one side, and the purpose of doing the right thing, on the other. We can be silly if we take everything for granted. But we can make a big deal out of the details of doing the right thing and forget *why* and what we're doing. That's why Mishnah ends as it does, with a powerful reminder of the main purpose of it all.

1. **What does it mean to be mindful? Why is this the most**

important thing Mishnah has to tell us?

2. Is it natural to be thankful? If it is, then why do we need rules about saying thanks? What is the purpose of rules for doing something that we do anyhow, without rules?

3. Why does Mishnah give us poems? How do the poems work?

4. Why does Mishnah talk about small and practical things? Wouldn't Mishnah be as helpful to us if it just made its main point? What purpose is there for all of the details?

5. What are the different kinds of food that Mishnah talks about? Why are these the important ones? Are these the same foods that we eat as our meals? If they're not, what are some of the things we eat all the time? Do you know the blessings you should say for those things?

6. Can you make up a Mishnah to cover the three things you regard as the most important things you eat every day? How will you construct it? What will you say in it? How will you know the right blessings to put into it? Can you also make up your own blessings in the model of the ones that Mishnah teaches us or takes for granted?

Wow!

MISHNAH BERAKHOT 9:2

Something about the blessings should bother you. We take for granted that a blessing is a way of saying thank you. But do you find the word *thanks* in the blessing? No. What you find in the blessing is the word *blessed.* When we bless something or someone, we may be doing any number of things. We may—as we know—mean to say thanks. But we may mean to say something else. To find out other things we mean when we say a blessing, consider other kinds of blessings. In *form* they are no different from the blessings we say over food, but in *substance* they are different.

Even though one of the most important things that happens to us is that we eat, that is not the only important thing. Something else happens to us and we should pay attention. What, in fact, are the things we *notice?* They are unusual things, things that are out of the ordinary. For these, too, we say blessings. But they are not blessings for the purpose of saying *thank you.* They are blessings for the purpose of saying, *Wow!*

What are the amazing things in the world? What are the things that attract your attention? And what are the things that Mishnah thinks are remarkable—are far out of the ordinary? Let's turn to the Mishnah that talks about the blessings we say for amazing things. The first thing we're going to see is that Mishnah wants us to notice unusual things. The second is that Mishnah wants us to acknowledge that God is doing these things, doing miracles and wonders every day. In saying a blessing for amazing things, we are stating that we know who it is who makes the wonders of everyday life. Mishnah wants us to be people who *think* and *thank,* who notice and exclaim, in all, people who are alert.

MISHNAH BERAKHOT 9:2

עַל הַזִּיקִין, וְעַל הַזְּוָעוֹת, וְעַל הַבְּרָקִים, וְעַל הָרְעָמִים, וְעַל
הָרוּחוֹת — אוֹמֵר 'בָּרוּךְ שֶׁכֹּחוֹ וּגְבוּרָתוֹ מָלֵא עוֹלָם'. עַל הֶהָרִים,
וְעַל הַגְּבָעוֹת, וְעַל הַיַּמִּים, וְעַל הַנְּהָרוֹת, וְעַל הַמִּדְבָּרוֹת — אוֹמֵר
'בָּרוּךְ עוֹשֵׂה מַעֲשֵׂה בְרֵאשִׁית'. רַבִּי יְהוּדָה אוֹמֵר: הָרוֹאֶה אֶת
הַיָּם הַגָּדוֹל אוֹמֵר 'בָּרוּךְ שֶׁעָשָׂה אֶת הַיָּם הַגָּדוֹל' — בִּזְמַן שֶׁרוֹאֶה
אוֹתוֹ לִפְרָקִים. עַל הַגְּשָׁמִים, וְעַל הַבְּשׂוֹרוֹת הַטּוֹבוֹת — אוֹמֵר
'בָּרוּךְ הַטּוֹב וְהַמֵּטִיב'; וְעַל שְׁמוּעוֹת רָעוֹת אוֹמֵר 'בָּרוּךְ דַּיַּן
הָאֱמֶת'.

Vocabulary

valleys	הַגְּבָעוֹת	shooting stars	הַזִּיקִין
seas	הַיַּמִּים	earthquakes	הַזְּוָעוֹת
rivers	הַנְּהָרוֹת	lightning	הַבְּרָקִים
deserts	הַמִּדְבָּרוֹת	thunder	הָרְעָמִים
work	מַעֲשֶׂה	storms	הָרוּחוֹת
when	בִּזְמַן	his power	כֹּחוֹ
occasionally	לִפְרָקִים	his might	גְבוּרָתוֹ
rains	הַגְּשָׁמִים	fill	מָלֵא
good news	בְּשׂוֹרוֹת טוֹבוֹת	world	עוֹלָם
bad news	שְׁמוּעוֹת רָעוֹת	mountains	הֶהָרִים

How the Mishnah Is Put Together

Over shooting stars	1 עַל הַזִּיקִין,
and over earthquakes	וְעַל הַזְּוָעוֹת,
and over lightning	וְעַל הַבְּרָקִים,

and over thunder	וְעַל הָרְעָמִים,
and over storms	וְעַל הָרוּחוֹת —
one says, Blessed (are you, Lord our God, ruler of the world,) whose power and might fill the whole world.	אוֹמֵר 'בָּרוּךְ שֶׁכֹּחוֹ וּגְבוּרָתוֹ מָלֵא עוֹלָם'.
Over mountains	2 עַל הֶהָרִים,
and over valleys	וְעַל הַגְּבָעוֹת,
and over oceans	וְעַל הַיַּמִּים,
and over rivers	וְעַל הַנְּהָרוֹת,
and over deserts	וְעַל הַמִּדְבָּרוֹת —
one says, Blessed (are you, Lord, our God, king of the world, who) makes the works of creation.	אוֹמֵר 'בָּרוּךְ עוֹשֶׂה מַעֲשֵׂה בְרֵאשִׁית'.
Rabbi Judah says,	3 רַבִּי יְהוּדָה אוֹמֵר:
He who sees the Great Sea (The Mediterranean) says	הָרוֹאֶה אֶת הַיָּם הַגָּדוֹל אוֹמֵר
Blessed (are you, Lord,) our God, king of the world, who made the Great Sea.	'בָּרוּךְ שֶׁעָשָׂה אֶת הַיָּם הַגָּדוֹל' —
(This is the case only) when one sees it from time to time (but not every day).	4 בִּזְמַן שֶׁרוֹאֶה אוֹתוֹ לִפְרָקִים.
Over rain	5 עַל הַגְּשָׁמִים,
and over good news	וְעַל הַבְּשׂוֹרוֹת הַטּוֹבוֹת —
one says, Blessed (are you, Lord, our God, ruler of the world) who is good and who does good things.	אוֹמֵר 'בָּרוּךְ הַטּוֹב וְהַמֵּטִיב';
And for bad news	וְעַל שְׁמוּעוֹת רָעוֹת

one says, Blessed (are you, Lord, our God, ruler of the world, who is) the true judge.

אוֹמֵר 'בָּרוּךְ דַּיַּן הָאֱמֶת'.

nce more, it's clear as day how the little poem has been put together. The first unit gives us five items, and the second one gives us five items, and the two obviously are matched—item for item. It's easy to memorize by fives because you have five fingers on your hand. What are the five things on each list?

The first five are unusual events. They are things that happen only once in a while. The second five, by contrast, are sights of nature. They are things you don't see every day unless you live near them, and they impress you when you do see them. Accordingly, we say different blessings for these different sorts of things. We'll come back to that point in a minute. First, let's finish seeing how the poem works.

Judah has a different opinion on one of the five items in No. 2. The Great Sea—the Mediterranean—has its own special blessing. That's not an important disagreement, of course, and it's just tacked on at the end of Nos. 1 and 2.

No. 4 tells us what we guessed, that we say these blessings in Nos. 3 and 4 once in a while—*only* when we see these mountains or valleys. After all, we can't spend all day staring at the mountain and saying a blessing over it—life doesn't work that way. That little phrase in No. 4 tells us something logical and correct, but which also is obvious. We call it a "gloss;" we add something, a phrase, a brief comment, to an already complete sentence.

No. 5 would be perfect except for its opening clause. Why would it be perfect? Because it has a perfect pair of thoughts: *Good news* against *bad news*. That's just what we have come to expect in poetry such as Mishnah's.

But someting breaks the poem up and spoils its match. It is the opening clause, "over rains." That clause obviously does not belong.

Is this poem easy to memorize? Of course it is. You just have to remember five things and match them with five others, then, at the end, remember two more things—a dozen in all. The words that spoil the pattern are still easier to remember! Now let's turn to what it means.

The first five things are what the weather report talks about, unusual events, what people call "weather." And the point Mishnah makes is that these unusual things tell us an important truth. God not only made the world. God *makes* the world even now. And the unusual and amazing things that happen are proof that God makes the world every day. They are evidence that God's might and power fill the whole world.

That is a deep idea, and Mishnah doesn't mince words saying it. If you want to know how great God is, how powerful God is, how awesome God is, then lift up your eyes to the heaven and see the stars. Open your ears in a great storm and hear the thunder. God is not the stars, and God is not the thunder. God *made* the stars and the thunder. They are evidence. They give testimony to God's great power. And so we say the blessing that is just as obvious, in its way, as the blessing for the fruit of the fruit-tree is in its way.

You remember how obvious that blessing was. All we say is *Blessed . . . who makes the fruit of the fruit-tree.* There isn't much more to be said than that. Here too, all we say is that these five things—and many like them—are things that remind us of the awesome power of God.

The next five are as ordinary as the first five are unusual. They are things that we don't see every day, and that amaze us just as much as thunder, a windstorm and lightning.

When we are surprised and awed by beautiful sights of nature—when we see the Grand Canyon or the Rocky Mountains of Colorado, the Wasach Front at Salt Lake City, Utah, or the White Mountains of New Hampshire, or when we gaze upon the Pacific Ocean from the Golden Gate, or when we stand on the bank of the Tennessee River in Knoxville, the Ohio in Cincinnati, the Mississippi in St. Louis or New Orleans, or when we look out on Lake Michigan from the Hancock Tower in Chicago, or on the vastness of the New York harbor from the World Trade Towers, or on the St. Lawrence at Montreal—when we see the great things that God has made, what do we say?

We say, "God made these things!" The blessing says no more than that—*Who makes the works of creation.*

Judah is not satisfied with that blessing for the Great Sea, the largest ocean he ever saw, the Mediterranean. He thinks there is a special blessing just for that—to him—the most unusual of all sights.

And then, in No. 4, we are told that these blessings are called for only when the sight is unusual, when it is not something you see every day. What does that mean? It means that we don't turn things into a habit. We don't even make saying a blessing a habit. We say a blessing only when it is not a habit, when it is something we use to express our surprise, wonder, amazement. Blessings are not routine and are not said in a sloppy way. They say something. They're not just mumbo-jumbo.

That brings us back to the blessings we say for food. Don't we say them all the time? True, we do. But we say those blessings only when we eat the particular foods that we mention, and those foods are not something we eat all day long. If we ate all day long, we wouldn't be wise to say blessings all day long. That would make a joke of saying a blessing. It is serious because a blessing is a way of saying, *Wow!* And, more, it's a way of saying, "My God! Did God do this for me? Thanks."

WHAT DOES IT MEAN TO ME?

The worst thing that can happen to you is to have too much—too many toys, too many exciting trips, too much cake. Because then you can't enjoy your toys, your trips, your cake. What kind of a life does a person have who has too much? It's a boring life. And that is the worst thing that can happen to you.

These blessings help us to see the exciting things all around us. They keep us alert to the wonders of nature, the excitement of, even, the weather. People who are bored with one another talk about the weather because they can't think of anything else to talk about. But when *we* talk about the weather, we *remember* something about it, and it's not a boring subject. We remember that God makes the world, even the rain, the thunder, the wind. And that the rain and thunder and wind testify to God's power in everything that happens.

110

The worst thing that can happen to you is to be blind to beautiful, wonderful things. If you visit a tremendous national park and get bored and forget what it all means, then that park, which should be your treasure and pleasure, is really nothing to you. People who are bored with themselves also are bored with the world around them. They don't notice what is happening around them. They don't even see the beautiful things in that world. There may be a beautiful sunset over the western hills, but they're inside, watching television. There may be a wonderful northeast wind blowing out from the bay or ocean that brings clear and clean air. But they're inside, nibbling on cookies. Then they don't seem to know that God is talking to them through the sunset and through the windstorm and telling them, "Look here! Notice me! These are things I do!"

That's where blessings come in. Because by reminding ourselves to say the right blessing, we also remember what the blessing says, which is what the wonderful thing, the thunder, the ocean, means, what it wants to say to us. These blessings are not little "rituals," something you do because you're supposed to. If you do them for reason of habit, you might be better off not doing them at all.

These blessings for the wind and for the sunset and for the mountains and for the hurricanes tell us:

1. God's power fills the world. God is reminding us of what that power actually is.

2. God is making the world *now,* making things happen *now.* "Creation" is not something that happened a long time ago. Creation is happening every minute. It's happening to you.

LET'S MAKE MISHNAH

It is now time for you to begin your own Mishnah. This is an especially good place to begin because this particular Mishnah is easy to imitate. We can imitate its form, can't we? All we need is a list of five things matched by another list of five things. We can find our own things too, once we know what is supposed to go on the list.

List five things that impress you in the natural world, five things that, in your mind, say one thing, which is that God is powerful and mighty.

Then of course you have to add your blessing at the end.

Now list five things that you might see from day to day, not necessarily something as general as "mountain" or "ocean," but something specific that is like "mountain" or "ocean." List things that impress you, that surprise you so much that you have to say a Jewish "wow"—a blessing that ends, "Who does the works of creation."

Try to match your five things line by line. Try to write them down in Hebrew. When you have them all in place—matching the form of Mishnah and matching the ideas of Mishnah—then don't you have a Mishnah? And didn't you make it yourself?

1. What is a blessing? What are the things we try to do by saying a blessing? Are all blessings for the same purpose?

2. Why is a blessing said for something usual such as eating? What do we say when we say a blessing over bread? What do we mean?

3. Why is a blessing said for something unusual, such as thunder or lightning? What do we say when we say a blessing for thunder? What do we mean?

4. What kind of people does Mishnah want us to be when it tells us to say blessings for these things? What is Mishnah's goal for us?

5. Why is it important that we remember to be surprised once in a while? Why is surprise the opposite of boredom?

6. Why does Judah think we need a special blessing when we see the largest ocean we know about (say the Pacific or Atlantic Oceans)? What are some other things for which, if Judah knew the world you live in, he would want to say a special blessing?

7. Why do we say a blessing when we hear good news? Why is it even more important to say a blessing when we hear bad news? What does Mishnah want to tell us by matching those two blessings together? Does Mishnah mean to say only that it's easy to remember things which come in pairs? Or does it have in mind some much deeper truth?

8. Why is it important to say the right blessing for the right

food or for the right natural event? What does Mishnah want to tell us by insisting that there are special blessings for special things? What kind of people does it want us to be by teaching us these lessons?

PART FOUR

Making Mishnah

Looking For Mishnah, Finding Torah

MISHNAH ABOT 2:8-9

You remember, a long time ago, we learned the Mishnah that tells the story of Mishnah: Moses received Torah from Sinai and he handed it on to Joshua, and so on. And we asked, "What is the *torah* of Mishnah?" What we've learned is that the *torah*—the truth, the teaching given by God—of Mishnah is the *torah* of the life we live every day. Mishnah is about everyday life and its *torah* is the *Torah* for everyday life.

Now let's finish by asking, "*How* do the great sages of Mishnah discover *torah* in everyday life? Where do they find it?"

We have two Mishnahs before us. In the first we learn about one of the greatest sages of Mishnah and about his students. We want to know, in particular, how this great sage and his students found the *torah* that they put into Mishnah. Where did they look for it? How did they look for it? When you know the answer to this question, you will understand the secret of Mishnah's *torah: Torah is to be found everywhere you look for it.* Because finding *torah* depends on the one who is looking for it. And making Mishnah is something anyone can do who *wants* to make Mishnah.

So let's see how the great sage of Mishnah teaches his students how to find *torah* and turn it into the oral Torah, Mishnah. To begin with, let me tell you the story of the man whom we're going to meet.

He is Yohanan ben Zakkai. Yohanan in English would be John. *Zakkai* means an upright man, someone who is fair and reliable. Sometimes *ben* means son, but sometimes it means "a person who has a certain quality." So *Yohanan ben Zakkai* could be called in English, "John the Upright" or "John the Fair." I tell you this so that Yohanan ben Zakkai's name does not make him seem like a strange person from another world. He really is someone you'd like to know. And when you hear the story of the man, you'll see why. Because Yohanan ben Zakkai is the man who saved the Torah at the time that the end of the world seemed to be at hand. What happened, and what did he do?

Our Mishnah tells us that he took over from Shammai and Hillel the work of handing on Torah. So he is an important person in the chain of tradition from Moses to us.

But he did something else which Mishnah also tells us, something equally important: he raised up important students, five in all. So his idea for keeping the Torah going was not only to take it over and hand it on to someone else, but to take it and give it to as many people as he could. And, as you'll see, he taught his students how to *find torah* for themselves, just as I've tried to teach you how to *find torah* for yourself.

But Yohanan ben Zakkai did a third thing. He saved the Torah from extinction. How did it happen?

A long time ago, in the beginning of the Common Era, the Jews and the Romans fought over the country called the Land of Israel, which today is the State of Israel. The Romans wanted to add the Land of Israel to their empire, and the Jews wanted to keep the Land of Israel for Israel, the Jewish people. And the very battlefield of the great war was Jerusalem, the holy city, and, in Jerusalem, the Temple, where the Jews worshipped God.

Now the war went badly for the Jews. And Yohanan ben Zakkai saw that the end was coming. He said, "Does this mean that the Torah must come to an end too? Will the loss of the Temple and the city, and even the Land itself, mean that Israel, the Jewish people, has nothing left in the world?"

"But at least part of Israel is going to live after the terrible calamity coming upon us. So I have to be sure that, whatever happens, Israel has Torah, Israel has a reason to live and has a *torah* that tells how to live.

"Because without Torah, even if Israel does outlive the Temple, the city, and even the Land, Israel is sure to die."

So Yohanan ben Zakkai decided that he had to go over to the Romans and make a deal with them so that Israel would not die even if it lost the Temple, the city and the Land. Because Israel would have the Torah.

Brave men were in charge of the city, and they believed that no one should leave. Everyone should stay and fight to the death. Death was all about. There was death in the battlefield, and people were starving to death in the streets, and there was sickness unto death in the homes. And the people in charge wanted to die rather than make a deal with the Romans. But Yohanan believed that the people of Israel must live for all time and at all cost.

117

What did Yohanan ben Zakkai do? He decided to go through the death that was everywhere and rise up beyond it. He did something symbolic. He took a coffin. And he lay down in it. And he said to his students, "Carry me out of the city as a corpse. Then the brave fighters will let me out, since they will think that I will have died, and they don't want to keep a corpse in the holy city."

So Yohanan ben Zakkai's students picked up the coffin in which he lay, and carried it to the gate. The guards, seeing that Yohanan ben Zakkai was in a coffin and supposing that he was dead, let the coffin out of the gates.

The students carried the coffin to the Roman camp, to the tent of the Roman general. He came out of the tent to see what was happening.

At that moment, as if rising from the dead, Yohanan ben Zakkai stood up from the coffin. He said, "Roman general, you are going to be the emperor of Rome. And when you are emperor, you will know that I told you so. Then you will grant me something, a small thing, which you won't even notice.

"It is to let me go to Yavneh (a little town near the coast of the Land of Israel where some refugees had found a safe place to live out the war), so that I and my students may study Torah and carry out the commandments and do deeds of kindness to other people."

"Now," the general thought, "what can be wrong with that? I have a war on my hands. This man wants peace. If he'll live peacefully under my rule, I'll let him do what he wants—study Torah."

So he gave Yohanan and his students permission to leave the scene of war and go to the quiet town of Yavneh. There they studied and kept the Torah alive so that, when all else would be lost—as indeed a couple of years later it was—the Torah would still be there.

Yohanan brought Israel from the death of war to the life of Torah. He himself—by lying down in the coffin and getting up again—died and came to life again. And what led him back to life was Torah.

This story speaks for itself. Now, let's turn back to Abot and see what it is that Yohanan ben Zakkai has to say in that important collection of wise sayings.

The Mishnah before us is in two parts. In the first part, Yohanan ben Zakkai tells us his important saying. We are created to study and do Torah.

Torah is our life. In the second part, we have a story about Yohanan and his students.

MISHNAH ABOT 2:8

רַבָּן יוֹחָנָן בֶּן זַכַּאי קִבֵּל מֵהִלֵּל וּמִשַּׁמַּאי. הוּא הָיָה אוֹמֵר:
אִם לָמַדְתָּ תוֹרָה הַרְבֵּה, אַל תַּחֲזִיק טוֹבָה לְעַצְמָךְ, כִּי לְכַךְ נוֹצָרְתָּ.

Vocabulary

received	קִבֵּל	for yourself	לְעַצְמָךְ
you learned	לָמַדְתָּ	because	כִּי
much	הַרְבֵּה	for this	לְכַךְ
do not	אַל	you were created	נוֹצָרְתָּ
hold onto	תַּחֲזִיק		

How the Mishnah Is Put Together

Rabban Yohanan ben Zakkai received (Torah) from Hillel and Shammai.	רַבָּן יוֹחָנָן בֶּן זַכַּאי קִבֵּל מֵהִלֵּל וּמִשַּׁמַּאי.
He would say	הוּא הָיָה אוֹמֵר:
If you have learned much Torah	אִם לָמַדְתָּ תוֹרָה הַרְבֵּה,
do not think well of yourself (on that account)	אַל תַּחֲזִיק טוֹבָה לְעַצְמָךְ,
for to that end were you created	כִּי לְכַךְ נוֹצָרְתָּ.

ohanan's saying is in three clauses, but it's all one saying. And what he tells you is something that you won't find surprising. He says, "If you've learned a lot of Torah, don't think you're something special—*because you too were made to learn torah.*"

You can't be especially proud to do what you're made to do. If you're a good athlete and can throw a ball into center field, why be proud of that? You're a good athlete. That's what you're supposed to do. If you're a good swimmer and can swim the butterfly stroke, well, your body is strong enough to do it. There's nothing special about that. And so, too, if you're a good singer, or if you're a good student in school. We are what we are. We do what we are made to do.

But Yohanan says this about *torah.* What does he mean? He means that it's perfectly natural for everyone to learn *torah,* to look for *torah* in the world because God made us into human beings who have eyes to see *torah* and ears to hear *torah* and minds to understand *torah.* Why? Because what is *torah,* if not what God tells us, and what God tells us is *truth.*

Yohanan's message is that *torah* is the one thing that is natural for us to learn. It may be hard to learn math or French or Hebrew, but it can't be hard to learn *torah.* And this leads us to the question: Where in the world does Yohanan want us to find *torah?* How does he want us to learn *torah?* Does he tell his students, "Now go look things up in books, and find out what is written in them?" Is that the 'learning much Torah' of which Yohanan speaks? I think you know the answer from the *torah* you already have learned. The Mishnahs you have studied are not about books but about things that happen to people, about things that happen to us every day. We don't have to repeat what you already know well.

There is *torah* to tell us what to do at every crossroads of life, every important decision we have to make about ourselves, about our life with our mothers and fathers and sisters and brothers, about our work with other people in school, about the games we play, about finding a penny on the street. Everything we have to decide can be a decision in line with *torah.* But the real thing we have to learn to do is to figure out the right decision.

And that is something we do with our own minds. We don't just go running to a book or to some great person—a rabbi, school principal, teacher, friend—and say, "What shall I do?" We have to decide for ourselves. And the way we decide, to begin with, is to learn how to make up our minds. And that means to learn to use our minds which God made in accord with Torah.

And you know full well that, in the Mishnahs you've been studying, you've been learning to use your mind the way God made it. That's why you learn Mishnah, and that's why you have been making your own Mishnah.

Now let's see what the students do to find Torah. First we notice that the students are told *Go*, meaning go out, and *See*, meaning look at things as they are. Yohanan doesn't say, "*Sit* here kids, and *listen* to what I say."

He says to them, "Go out there and look around. Use your eyes. Think about what you see. And then come back and tell me the right from the wrong answer."

And here are the answers.

MISHNAH ABOT 2:8,9

חֲמִשָּׁה תַלְמִידִים הָיוּ לְרַבָּן יוֹחָנָן בֶּן זַכַּאי, וְאֵלּוּ הֵן: רַבִּי אֱלִיעֶזֶר בֶּן הֻרְקָנוֹס, וְרַבִּי יְהוֹשֻׁעַ בֶּן חֲנַנְיָה, וְרַבִּי יוֹסֵי הַכֹּהֵן, וְרַבִּי שִׁמְעוֹן בֶּן נְתַנְאֵל, וְרַבִּי אֶלְעָזָר בֶּן עֲרָךְ.

אָמַר לָהֶם: צְאוּ וּרְאוּ אֵיזוֹהִי דֶרֶךְ יְשָׁרָה שֶׁיִּדְבַּק בָּהּ הָאָדָם. רַבִּי אֱלִיעֶזֶר אוֹמֵר: עַיִן טוֹבָה. רַבִּי יְהוֹשֻׁעַ אוֹמֵר: חָבֵר טוֹב. רַבִּי יוֹסֵי אוֹמֵר: שָׁכֵן טוֹב. רַבִּי שִׁמְעוֹן אוֹמֵר: הָרוֹאֶה אֶת הַנּוֹלָד. רַבִּי אֶלְעָזָר אוֹמֵר: לֵב טוֹב. אָמַר לָהֶם: רוֹאֶה אֲנִי אֶת דִּבְרֵי אֶלְעָזָר בֶּן עֲרָךְ, שֶׁבִּכְלַל דְּבָרָיו דִּבְרֵיכֶם. אָמַר לָהֶם: צְאוּ וּרְאוּ אֵיזוֹהִי דֶרֶךְ רָעָה שֶׁיִּתְרַחֵק מִמֶּנָּה הָאָדָם. רַבִּי אֱלִיעֶזֶר אוֹמֵר: עַיִן רָעָה. רַבִּי יְהוֹשֻׁעַ אוֹמֵר: חָבֵר רַע. רַבִּי יוֹסֵי אוֹמֵר: שָׁכֵן רַע. רַבִּי שִׁמְעוֹן אוֹמֵר: הַלֹּוֶה וְאֵינוֹ מְשַׁלֵּם. רַבִּי אֶלְעָזָר אוֹמֵר: לֵב רַע. אָמַר לָהֶם: רוֹאֶה אֲנִי אֶת דִּבְרֵי אֶלְעָזָר בֶּן עֲרָךְ, שֶׁבִּכְלַל דְּבָרָיו דִּבְרֵיכֶם.

Vocabulary

five	חֲמִשָּׁה	neighbor	שָׁכֵן
disciples	תַּלְמִידִים	the future	הַנּוֹלָד
go out	צְאוּ	heart	לֵב
what	אֵיזוֹהִי	words (of)	דִּבְרֵי
good way	דֶּרֶךְ יְשָׁרָה	evil way	דֶּרֶךְ רָעָה
cling to	יִדְבַּק	stay away from	יִתְרַחֵק
man	הָאָדָם	he who borrows	הַלֹּוֶה
eye	עַיִן	pay back	מְשַׁלֵּם
friend	חָבֵר		

How the Mishnah Is Put Together

Five students did Rabban Yohanan ben Zakkai have and these are they:	1 חֲמִשָּׁה תַלְמִידִים הָיוּ לְרַבָּן יוֹחָנָן בֶּן זַכַּאי, וְאֵלוּ הֵן:
Rabbi Eliezer ben Hyrcanus	רַבִּי אֱלִיעֶזֶר בֶּן הוֹרְקָנוֹס,
Rabbi Joshua ben Hananiah	וְרַבִּי יְהוֹשֻׁעַ בֶּן חֲנַנְיָה,
Rabbi Yose the priest	וְרַבִּי יוֹסֵי הַכֹּהֵן,
Rabbi Simeon ben Netanel	וְרַבִּי שִׁמְעוֹן בֶּן נְתַנְאֵל,
Rabbi Eleazar ben Arakh	וְרַבִּי אֶלְעָזָר בֶּן עֲרָךְ.
He said to them	2 אָמַר לָהֶם:
Go out and see: What is the straight path to which man should cleave	צְאוּ וּרְאוּ אֵיזוֹהִי דֶּרֶךְ יְשָׁרָה שֶׁיִּדְבַּק בָּהּ הָאָדָם.
Rabbi Eliezer says, A good eye.	רַבִּי אֱלִיעֶזֶר אוֹמֵר: עַיִן טוֹבָה.
Rabbi Joshua says, A good friend.	רַבִּי יְהוֹשֻׁעַ אוֹמֵר: חָבֵר טוֹב.

Rabbi Yose says, A good neighbor.	רַבִּי יוֹסֵי אוֹמֵר: שָׁכֵן טוֹב.
Rabbi Simeon says, He who sees what is going to happen (foresight)	רַבִּי שִׁמְעוֹן אוֹמֵר: הָרוֹאֶה אֶת הַנּוֹלָד.
Rabbi Eleazar says, A good heart.	רַבִּי אֶלְעָזָר אוֹמֵר: לֵב טוֹב.
He said to them, I regard the opinion of Eleazar ben Arakh (as superior).	אָמַר לָהֶם: רוֹאֶה אֲנִי אֶת דִּבְרֵי אֶלְעָזָר בֶּן עֲרָךְ,
For contained in his opinion are your opinions.	שֶׁבִּכְלַל דְּבָרָיו דִּבְרֵיכֶם.
He said to them	3 אָמַר לָהֶם:
Go out and see: What is the bad path, from which man should keep far.	צְאוּ וּרְאוּ אֵיזוֹהִי דֶּרֶךְ רָעָה שֶׁיִּתְרַחֵק מִמֶּנָּה הָאָדָם.
Rabbi Eliezer says, A bad eye.	רַבִּי אֱלִיעֶזֶר אוֹמֵר: עַיִן רָעָה.
Rabbi Joshua says, A bad friend.	רַבִּי יְהוֹשֻׁעַ אוֹמֵר: חָבֵר רַע.
Rabbi Yose says, A bad neighbor.	רַבִּי יוֹסֵי אוֹמֵר: שָׁכֵן רַע.
Rabbi Simeon says, He who borrows but does not pay back.	רַבִּי שִׁמְעוֹן אוֹמֵר: הַלֹּוֶה וְאֵינוּ מְשַׁלֵּם.
Rabbi Eleazar says, A bad heart.	רַבִּי אֶלְעָזָר אוֹמֵר: לֵב רַע.
He said to them, I regard the opinion of Eleazar ben Arakh (as superior).	אָמַר לָהֶם: רוֹאֶה אֲנִי אֵב דִּבְרֵי אֶלְעָזָר בֶּן עֲרָךְ,
For contained in his opinion are your opinions.	שֶׁבִּכְלַל דְּבָרָיו דִּבְרֵיכֶם.

irst we notice that, as usual, everything is carefully arranged like a little poem. Each of our three parts—Nos. 1, 2 and 3—is composed of a sentence that tells us what's going on, the names of the five students, together with what they say (for Nos. 2 and 3). At the end of the last two parts, we see Yohanan's opinion of what the students tell him.

Let's proceed directly to five things that the five students say in answer to Yohanan's two questions (ten things in all, as usual!)

Yohanan asks, "What is the right way, which a person should follow?" And he asks, "What is the wrong way, which a person should avoid?" And the five students say one thing in No. 2, then its opposite in No. 3 (except for Simeon—his sayings don't match). So we have:

1. good eye, and bad eye
2. good friend, and bad friend
3. good neighbor, and bad neighbor
4. foresight, and borrowing and not paying back (which is the opposite of foresight)
5. good heart, bad heart.

Let's begin.

Eliezer says how you regard other people is the most important. A "good eye" is a generous person, one who sees that other people have good things and is not jealous. A "bad eye" is a selfish, mean person, who sees that other people have good things and is jealous for that reason. Joshua and Yose are telling almost the same thing. If you want to be a good person, stick around good people. Avoid bad friends, who lead you into bad ways. Simeon has a different idea. What's important to him is to have an idea of what is going to happen. You may remember that, when we talked about making vows, we said that a person can get out of a vow (in Eliezer's opinion) if he says, "I didn't foresee that thing." Here, too, Simeon says that the most important thing a person should do is to try to figure out what is going to happen. This means, especially, to figure out what will happen if you do a

124

certain thing, and what will not happen if you do some other thing. And, on the opposite side, he says the worst things you can do is borrow and not pay back. If you borrow, you should know that you're going to have the money to pay back. If you don't have the money to pay back, it means that you borrowed "without foresight."

And then comes Eleazar ben Arakh. Why is the matter of the *heart* so important to Eleazar? You can construct the answer to that question out of the Mishnahs you have learned. In fact, what Eleazar says is something you already know. It is:

Everything depends upon your thought, your attitude, your intention—which are included in the word—"heart." If you think back to the many points in our learning of Mishnah at which your attitude is the most important, decisive thing, you will realize how right Yohanan is to say: "Eleazar's opinion takes in everyone else's opinion."

We don't have to expand much on this point, because it simply says, in a general way, something you already know in many concrete ways. Instead, let's go back to find out, where do the Yohanan's students learn the lessons that they bring back to their teacher? The most important words in the Mishnah before us are buried in the introduction: *Go and see.*

Let's talk about the part that says *go.* Where do the students learn Mishnah? They learn it in school, of course, with Yohanan. But they seek *torah* in the streets, in the playgrounds, in all the places where they live when they're not in school. So Yohanan tells the students to go outside the school, the place of learning, to learn *torah.*

And the second word—*see*—is equally important. He doesn't tell his students to ask people what is good or what is bad. He tells them to observe, to watch what people do and what happens as a result, to come to their own judgments and make up their own minds—and then to come back to school and work things out for the purposes of Mishnah-learning.

So these two things go together: 1. Go *outside* and 2. *see* what can be seen. And yet, there is the unstated fact that the students *do* come back and report to Yohanan what they learn. Yohanan then takes their observations, the things they have seen on the outside, and puts them into Mishnah and makes them part of the oral Torah which God reveals to Moses at Mount Sinai.

1. What examples, among the Mishnahs you have learned, il-

lustrate the idea that Mishnah is about everyday life? In what ways does Mishnah speak of everyday life a long time ago? In what ways does Mishnah speak of everyday life today? How can you remake Mishnah into something which is relevant to your own world?

2. What trade did Yohanan ben Zakkai make with the Roman general? What do you think the soldiers of his time thought of the trade? Why do you think that Yohanan did the wrong thing?

3. Why does Yohanan ben Zakkai say that you should not be proud if you learn a lot of Torah? Can you say that you shouldn't be proud if you hit many home runs? What attitude does he think you should have about your abilities? What does he think is natural for the people of Israel? Is he right? Do Jewish people you know take for granted their real purpose in life is to learn Torah?

4. In what ways is it natural to learn Torah? What connection do you see between learning Torah and living life?

5. Why were Yohanan ben Zakkai's students so important to him? Do you notice that, when the Mishnah wants to tell us what was important about Yohanan, it lists the names of his students? Do you think you're that important to your teachers? Why did Yohanan think that his students were the most important thing anyone could know about himself or herself?

6. What is so important about a 'good eye' or a 'bad eye'? What do you think Eliezer had in mind by saying that one's attitude toward other people was the most important thing in life?

7. What is so important about a good friend or a bad friend, a good neighbor or a bad neighbor? Why did Joshua tell Yohanan that the best thing you can do is have the right kind of friend?

8. What is so important about foresight—about trying to figure out what is going to happen? Why does Simeon then say the worst thing you can do is borrow from someone else and

126

not pay back?

9. Eleazar ben Arakh speaks of a good heart and a bad heart. How would you put into your own words what Eleazar ben Arakh was talking about?

10. Why do you think Yohanan told his students to go out and see what they could see? Shouldn't he have told them to read the written Torah or in other holy books to find out what is good and what is bad? What attitude does Yohanan express toward the place where truth is found?

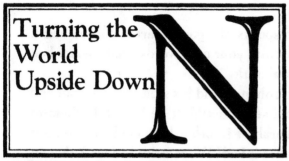

Turning the World Upside Down

MISHNAH ABOT 4:1

Now you must ask, "If my teacher told me to walk out into the street and bring back *torah*, what should I look for?" Because if you want to make Mishnah yourself, you probably would like to learn more Mishnah than the handful we have learned together. And the two go together. If you learn Mishnah, it teaches you how to see things. When you do see things, then you have something you want to add to Mishnah. Mishnah is like a new pair of glasses. It changes your view of things. It helps you to see things in a new way. And once you do, nothing is ever the same.

What secret can you learn from Mishnah that will change your view of everything?

To answer that question, we're going to learn one last Mishnah, a strange, mysterious and beautiful one. Because its message to us is that things are *not* what they seem. In fact, things are often the opposite of what they seem to be. And when you learn to see that strange vision, then you will agree with Simeon that the most important thing is to see what is going to be. And you'll agree with Joshua about the good neighbor and with Eliezer about the 'good eye'—about generosity and good will toward other people. And, above all, you'll see why Yohanan says that Eleazar's view of the importance of the good heart takes in everyone else's ideas.

MISHNAH ABOT 4:1

בֶּן זוֹמָא אוֹמֵר: אֵיזֶהוּ הֶחָכָם? הַלּוֹמֵד מִכָּל אָדָם, שֶׁנֶּאֱמַר:

'מִכָּל מְלַמְּדַי הִשְׂכַּלְתִּי'. אֵיזֶהוּ גִבּוֹר? הַכּוֹבֵשׁ אֶת יִצְרוֹ, שֶׁנֶּאֱמַר:

'טוֹב אֶרֶךְ אַפַּיִם מִגִּבּוֹר וּמֹשֵׁל בְּרוּחוֹ מִלֹּכֵד עִיר'. אֵיזֶהוּ עָשִׁיר?

הַשָּׂמֵחַ בְּחֶלְקוֹ, שֶׁנֶּאֱמַר: 'יְגִיעַ כַּפֶּיךָ כִּי תֹאכֵל אַשְׁרֶיךָ וְטוֹב לָךְ'.

אַשְׁרֶיךָ — בָּעוֹלָם הַזֶּה, וְטוֹב לָךְ — לָעוֹלָם הַבָּא. אֵיזֶהוּ מְכֻבָּד?

הַמְכַבֵּד אֶת הַבְּרִיּוֹת, שֶׁנֶּאֱמַר: 'כִּי מְכַבְּדַי אֲכַבֵּד וּבֹזַי יֵקָלּוּ'.

Vocabulary

who	אֵיזֶהוּ	city	עִיר
wise	חָכָם	rich	עָשִׁיר
he who learns	הַלּוֹמֵד	he who is happy	הַשָּׂמֵחַ
from every	מִכָּל	his portion	חֶלְקוֹ
man	אָדָם	labor	יְגִיעַ
as it is written	שֶׁנֶּאֱמַר	your hands	כַּפֶּיךָ
I have learned	הִשְׂכַּלְתִּי	you shall eat	תֹאכֵל
mighty	גִּבּוֹר	you are happy	אַשְׁרֶיךָ
he who subdues	הַכּוֹבֵשׁ	this world	עוֹלָם הַזֶּה
his (evil) nature	יִצְרוֹ	world to come	עוֹלָם הַבָּא
good	טוֹב	honored	מְכֻבָּד
slow to anger	אֶרֶךְ אַפַּיִם	mankind	הַבְּרִיּוֹת
manages	וּמֹשֵׁל	those who despise me	בֹּזַי
his spirit	רוּחוֹ	will be esteemed	יֵקָלוּ
seize	לִכֵד	lightly	

HOW OUR MISHNAH WORKS

This is an important Mishnah to memorize. When you know this by heart, it is going to ring in your ears, and you won't be able to put it out of your mind. It's like a bell, clanging all the time. No matter where you go, you hear it.

Let's take the Mishnah apart, and see how it is put together.

Ben Zoma says,	בֶּן זוֹמָא אוֹמֵר:

Who is a wise person? The one who learns from everybody	1 אֵיזֶהוּ חָכָם? הַלּוֹמֵד מִכָּל אָדָם,
As it is said (in the written Torah) I have learned from all my teachers	שֶׁנֶּאֱמַר: 'מִכָּל מְלַמְּדַי הִשְׂכַּלְתִּי'.
Who is the strong person? The one who overcomes his impulse	2 אֵיזֶהוּ גִבּוֹר? הַכּוֹבֵשׁ אֶת יִצְרוֹ,
As it is said, He who is slow to anger is better than the strong man, and he who controls his mood than the one who captures a city	שֶׁנֶּאֱמַר: 'טוֹב אֶרֶךְ אַפַּיִם מִגִּבּוֹר וּמֹשֵׁל בְּרוּחוֹ מִלֹּכֵד עִיר'.
Who is rich? The one who is contented with what he has	3 אֵיזֶהוּ עָשִׁיר? הַשָּׂמֵחַ בְּחֶלְקוֹ,
As it is said, You shall eat the fruit of the labor of your hands, you shall be happy, and it shall be well with you.	שֶׁנֶּאֱמַר: 'יְגִיעַ כַּפֶּיךָ כִּי תֹאכֵל אַשְׁרֶיךָ וְטוֹב לָךְ'.
You shall be happy— in this world;	אַשְׁרֶיךָ — בָּעוֹלָם הַזֶּה,
and it shall be well with you— in the world to come.	4 וְטוֹב לָךְ — לָעוֹלָם הַבָּא.
Who is honored? The person who honors other people,	אֵיזֶהוּ מְכֻבָּד? הַמְכַבֵּד אֶת הַבְּרִיּוֹת,
As it is said, For those who honor me I honor, and those who despise me shall be despised	שֶׁנֶּאֱמַר: 'כִּי מְכַבְּדַי אֲכַבֵּד וּבֹזַי יֵקָלּוּ'.

f course this Mishnah is put together so clearly that we scarcely need to comment on it. Ben Zoma has four sayings. Each saying asks a question and answers it simply. Then—and this is new for us—each saying is accompanied by a quotation from the written Torah. We'll spend some time on that side of matters because it completes our journey into the part of the Torah that is memorized.

What is it that Ben Zoma does? In each case, he takes a basic quality—wisdom, power, wealth, honor—things everyone wants, and he turns it on its head.

Real wisdom, real power, real wealth, real honor—these are not what people think they are. In fact, if you don't know that what people think is right is wrong, and what people think is wrong is right, then you don't really know what wealth, wisdom, power and honor are. That is Ben Zoma's basic point.

How does he spell it out? He asks, "Who is a wise man?" Now ordinary folk are likely to say, "Someone who knows a great deal." "But that is not the point of wisdom," Ben Zoma answers you. No way. The point of wisdom is to *learn* from everyone. If you learn what everyone knows, if you *ask* people instead of *telling* people, then you really learn, and that is what makes you wise. So wisdom is not to show off for other people what *you* know but to learn from them what *they* know.

This is shrewd. After all, when you tell many things to other people, what are you learning? Nothing. You're just repeating what *you* know. You learn when you listen to other people talk. So what Ben Zoma says is the opposite of what you'd expect—and yet, when you think about it, it is absolutely right.

Who is strong? Is it someone who can control many things, who can lift weights, who can run the fastest, who can push through a crowd? No way. The strong person controls what takes strength to control. And strength, Ben Zoma says, has more than one meaning. True, strength is what lifts weights. But strength is something inside you, too. And what takes more strength—in the sense of having control or power over something—than controlling your own impulses? That is true strength. Few people have it.

What does Ben Zoma do here? He takes a word that people think means one thing, and he makes it mean something else—which people immediately recognize is right. It's clever on his part, and, when you think about it, it's absolutely correct. Because, as you well know, it's easier to control the path of a soccer ball than it is to control your temper.

Who is rich? The obvious answer is someone who has a lot of money and many things. But you know that people who have a lot still want more. Nothing is so unsatisfying as too much cheese cake or too much ice cream. When you've had all you want, you realize there's no limit to what you want. And who has not heard of the poor little rich kid who has everything in the world but loving parents and good friends? So riches must mean something more, and something else.

This is Ben Zoma's point: to be rich is to have whatever you want. But to be truly rich is to know what you need. The wealthy person is the person who has everything—everything he or she wants. That is what it means to be rich, and anyone can be rich. But people with a lot of money are not necessarily rich at all.

Then comes honor. What is honor? It's the sense that people respect you and look up to you. Now if you say, "Who is really honored?" What answer do you expect? Someone who is captain of the baseball team, or who is president of the class? No way. The person who is honored is the one who respects other people. This is true for two reasons.

First, if you don't respect other people, you don't respect yourself.

Second, it is simply not likely that people will respect you if you don't respect them. If you respect other people, you bring out their good qualities and make them want to respect you. After all, you have done something important for them. And if you respect other people, it shows you respect yourself. Once people know that you take yourself seriously, they will take you seriously and honor you.

So there is a certain irony in everything Ben Zoma says. That is, he turns everything upside down. But there also is a certain practical truth in what he says. Because what he tells you is simply what you must do to have the things you want. And, finally, there is a certain wisdom in what he says.

It adds up to this: everything depends on you. You have to be for yourself. You have to be for other people. And you have to do it now. This is the famous saying of Hillel.

Now let's turn back to something odd in Ben Zoma's saying. At each point, he quotes a verse of the written Torah. Let's go back over these verses and see what they say and why Ben Zoma quotes them.

The first, which proves that you should learn from everyone, is "I have learned from all my teachers" (Psalm 119:99). That seems clear enough. Ben Zoma agrees with the written Torah.

And to prove that the strong man is the one who overcomes his impulses, Ben Zoma cites Proverbs 16:32: "He who is slow to anger is better than the strong man, and he who controls his spirit than the one who captures a city." Scripture here, too, says exactly what Mishnah says through Ben Zoma.

To prove that the rich man is the one who is satisfied with what he has, Ben Zoma cites Psalm 128:2, "You shall eat the fruit of the labor of your hands, you shall be happy, and it shall be well with you." There doesn't seem to be much difference between the written Torah and the oral Torah.

And, finally, Mishnah ties up Ben Zoma's saying on the honored person's being the one who honors other people to I Samuel 2:30: "For those who honor me I shall honor, and those who despise me shall be despised." It is God who speaks here. The point, for Ben Zoma's purpose, is that those who give honor are honored, and those who pay contempt are despised.

So it would seem clear that everything Ben Zoma wants to say he can find in the written Torah. That is important to us for a simple reason.

We began our work by learning that the Torah is in two parts, written and oral. The Scriptures, the Five Books of Moses written in the Torah scroll we carry around the synagogue and sing on Shabbat morning, the Prophets and the Writings—these are only half of the Torah. The other half is Mishnah, the foundation of the oral Torah. So at the end of our study of oral Torah it is important for Ben Zoma to remind us that the written Torah stands behind the oral Torah, and the oral Torah stands behind the written Torah. The whole Torah of Moses our rabbi is one Torah, in two parts. Each part has its place and its purpose. But each part is complete and whole only with the other.

The insight we have learned from the oral Torah is to be discovered in the written Torah, just as the great teachings of the written Torah are to be found in the oral Torah. The reason is simple. God gave one Torah to Israel —one Torah for all of life, one Torah to keep us alive.

WHAT DOES IT MEAN TO ME?

Now let's ask, "How shall we make Mishnah?" The answer is simple because we've been making Mishnah for many months. There are four steps.

1. You have to think of an important question, a question that is so urgent you simply have to find the answer. If you have no questions, then Mishnah has no answers. And no Mishnah you can make can answer any questions for anyone else—so don't bother.

But surely there are important questions, like, What should I do on a date? Or, How shall I act toward my little brother and sister? Or, What do I owe to my parents? Or, Why should I keep Shabbat? Or, How shall I behave in school? Or, What kinds of friends do I want?

2. You have to open your eyes and look at the world and see what happens when people do one thing, what happens when they do another. And you have to collect these facts of what happens in the world and try to see some sort of repeated pattern, some truth which governs all kinds of actions.

3. And you have to try to see whether, in the one whole Torah, you can find relevant stories or sayings about the same problem. If there are no answers to your questions, there will be answers to questions like your questions. It's a matter of learning how to learn and listen.

4. But since this is your Mishnah, too, you have to make up words to capture the insight, the truth that you have found. You know that Mishnah is made up so that it is easy to memorize. So you, too, should find some pattern of words that is easy to memorize, some pattern of words that captures the pattern of life you have seen.

Who is a true sportsman?

One who is a good sport.

That's one example that shows us how easy it is to follow the example of Ben Zoma—both in the way he says what he wants to say and in what he tells us.

Or you can make a list of important things: *These are the things that one may do on a date,* list ten things and *These are the things that one may not do on a date,* list ten things. These of course are examples of how easy it is to follow the simple and memorable way Mishnah makes words work for itself.

The real goal is to make your own what Mishnah wants to give you. To do so, everything depends upon your heart, upon your attitude. You really do control your own life and your own destiny—if you realize that what is at the bottom of things is your own attitude, the way you express your true self. So to begin with, the questions you should take out of this book and into the world are: What do I think about this? What do I *want* to do about this? How do I want things to be? And that is how I shall make them be.

1. Why is it important to look for <u>torah</u> in the street? Is this how God made things?

2. Why are things the opposite of what they seem? Is that really what Ben Zoma wants to say? But is that always true? What is Ben Zoma's really <u>new</u> idea?

3. Thinking the way Ben Zoma does, can you ask an important question and answer it? For instance, "Who is popular?" "Who is beautiful?" or "Who is handsome?" What sort of answers would Ben Zoma give?

4. Why are the superficial answers people usually give to these kinds of questions usually wrong? What point do people miss?

5. Are "riches" as people generally define "riches," the same thing as what Ben Zoma talks about? Or has he really changed the meaning of the words he uses?

6. Why does Ben Zoma think it important to tie up his definitions to the teachings of the written Torah? Isn't it enough to say them in such a way that they are obviously true? What does the written Torah add to Ben Zoma's saying?

7. Why do we regard the two Torahs as one whole Torah? Why is one not complete without the other?

8. What are "important questions" that you simply must an-

swer? Where do you find such urgent questions? How do you go about looking for them?

9. Why is it useful to copy the way Mishnah says things? Isn't it easier to say them in our own words? Why do poems and patterns of words help us?

10. Can you think of ways in which your attitude toward something makes all the difference in the world?

Printed in the USA
CPSIA information can be obtained
at www.ICGtesting.com
JSHW052018140824
68134JS00027B/2537